Other Books in the Alice Nestleton Mystery Series

A Cat on the Bus

An Alice Nestleton Mystery

Lydia Adamson

A SIGNET BOOK

SIGNET
Published by New American Library, a division of
Penguin Putnam Inc., 375 Hudson Street,
New York, New York 10014, U.S.A.
Penguin Books Ltd, 80 Strand,
London WC2R 0RL, England
Penguin Books Australia Ltd, Ringwood,
Victoria, Australia
Penguin Books Canada Ltd, 10 Alcorn Avenue,
Toronto, Ontario, Canada M4V 3B2
Penguin Books (N.Z.) Ltd, 182–190 Wairau Road,
Auckland 10, New Zealand

Penguin Books Ltd, Registered Offices:
Harmondsworth, Middlesex, England

Published by Signet, an imprint of New American Library,
a division of Penguin Putnam Inc.

First Printing, December 2002
10 9 8 7 6 5 4 3 2 1

 REGISTERED TRADEMARK—MARCA REGISTRADA

Printed in the United States of America

PUBLISHER'S NOTE
This is a work of fiction. Names, characters, places, and incidents either
are the product of the author's imagination or are used fictitiously, and
any resemblance to actual persons, living or dead, business establish-
ments, events, or locales is entirely coincidental.

Chapter 1

What a difference a season makes. And winter was always my season.

I was on my way to the annual midwinter one-day sample sale at Eileen Fisher. Not, mind you, at one of the uptown branches, nor the lower Fifth Avenue store, nor the one on West Broadway. No, I patronize the East Village extension, on Ninth Street, between First and Second avenues.

The store opens at 10 A.M. on the day of the sale, so I was at the stop for the crosstown bus—the M8—on Washington and Tenth Street by nine-thirty.

I felt fine for several reasons. First of all, I was going to a sale at my favorite clothing store. I was flush, as the saying goes, and to use another cliché, the money was burning a hole in my pocket.

Second, the money in my pocket might last for a while, since I had landed a role in a new cable TV series called *Mulberry Street*. It was a knockoff of the wildly successful *The Sopranos*. And while just a little less ridiculous than the original, it paid quite well. My role? A bit sad for a graduate of the Tyrone Guthrie Theatre and the Dramatic Workshop and a twenty-year veteran of high-toned avant garde Off-Broadway productions: I was Angela, an old mafia gun moll returning home to settle scores.

Given my new wealth and my busy schedule, I had suspended my professional cat-sitting career.

I had a couple of other reasons for feeling good: A.G. Roth had decided not to return from England, and Tony Basillio was still in Los Angeles three months after he was supposed to have come home.

Both A.G. and Basillio were in the old-fashioned sense difficult beaus . . . so it was bye-bye and good riddance to both of them.

And a new beau was emerging fast. Very fast.

Yes, it had been a rather lively winter so far.

I was the only passenger on the M8 when it left Washington Street on its long route eastward from Greenwich Village to the farthest reaches of the East Village. I went all the way to the rear of the bus and sat down on the long seat, the one over the engine, which, as everyone knows, is the warmest spot.

Three more riders got on at Hudson Street.

At Seventh Avenue at least five boarded, including a plain-looking young woman with a cat carrier in one hand and a shopping bag in the other. She sat down two seats away from me, placing the bag on the floor and the carrier in her lap. She was wearing fur-lined boots, jeans, an Irish fisherman's sweater, and a long plaid muffler. Her hair was brown, cut short and shaggy. She wore only a trace of a very light shade of lipstick.

She was not only plain but shy-seeming. She gave me an apologetic smile—maybe for taking up so much space with her packages.

The cat in the carrier was silent. All I could see were his ears shifting and his eyes glaring, if indeed it was a "he."

I couldn't make out what breed of cat it was.

The writing on the shopping bag was quite clear—METROPOLITAN MUSEUM OF ART GIFT SHOP— but the bag was worn.

There did seem to be many small objects in the bag, freshly gift-wrapped. But Christmas was long gone.

Perhaps, I thought, she teaches in a private school and she's going on her winter break and the gifts are belated Christmas presents for her colleagues; maybe she had the flu over the holiday season. As for the cat—well, I told myself, she might be bringing that animal in to show her class before the vacation because she always talks to the children about her feline friend.

I always play this game on buses, trying to imagine the age, occupation, home life, and general disposition of fellow travelers. In this case I had the feeling I wasn't even close to the reality, mainly because the woman had struck me as being plain when she boarded the bus and I had learned that women one considers plain are usually faking plainness.

At Fifth Avenue the bus started to get crowded.

I closed my yes and thought of Lester Rawls. His role in *Mulberry Street* was that of mob lawyer. When I said I was involved with a new beau, I meant Lester, though, to be honest, it was a bit early to describe the relationship between us as an involvement. I mean, the real involvement had not yet started. Not yet the intimacy, or the affair, or . . . call it what you will.

But the fire was lit.

Lester and I talked, joked, had coffee together. We had those silly, cynical conversations that actors on the set of an embarrassing production have when each is trying to assure the other he or she won't be judged by this role.

I really liked the way Lester Rawls looked and talked and moved. I even liked the way he acted.

He had close-cropped, prematurely gray hair. He was on the short side, and he was strong, and he walked with this weird kind of spring in his step, as if he were about to leap. He had the most wonderful voice. I had never heard a dialect of American English quite like this before, and I consider myself something of an expert on such things. I have been known to identify the county of origin of California actresses after hearing them speak just ten lines.

It turned out that Lester was born and raised on Cape Cod.

A sound from the plain woman on the bus brought me out of the Rawls reverie.

I stared at her. She was speaking to me. "Are we close to the Broadway stop?" she asked.

I leaned over and held up two fingers. "First comes University Place and then Broadway."

She nodded her thanks.

The bus pulled into the University Place stop. I stared at the Taiwanese restaurant on the corner. It had always fascinated me, but I had never eaten there. The menu was incredibly complex and five pages long, with all kinds of appetizers I had never even heard of. It was country cuisine, the menu said, from the Taiwanese mountains. A lot of pig parts with exotic root vegetables.

The bus pulled away from the curb and headed on eastward.

The woman with the shopping bag and cat carrier stood up, pressed the overhead tape to signal a stop, and walked to the exit door with her packages.

I felt a sudden affection for the stranger. She exited a bus in the same prudent manner I did: Ring the signal a block before you stop. Bring yourself and all packages to the exit door. Wait patiently.

Yes, I liked the woman's bus style.

We reached Broadway. The bus slid into the stop at the curb.

The green light on the exit door went on.

The woman pressed the door strip and stepped down. The doors swung open and she stepped off.

At least I thought she did—until I heard the driver call out: "Will somebody please get the back door."

I looked. The back door light was still on. The doors hadn't closed automatically, as they should have, after the plain woman stepped off the bus.

But it wasn't a malfunction. She had not really exited at all. She was still there, standing on the bottom step, her body squarely between the doors.

Then she stepped back into the bus, placing the cat carrier and the shopping bag on the top step.

It occurred to me that she believed it was the wrong stop. But she had asked me about Broadway and this certainly was Broadway.

Then she bent and reached into her shopping bag, pulling out a smaller paper bag. This one she ripped open.

A pistol emerged.

She pointed the large dull weapon, released the safety, and fired four times. The object spat iron as if the woman had burped it.

Bullets struck passengers seated directly across from the back door.

People began to scream. The woman dropped the weapon back into the large shopping bag and calmly walked off, leaving the cat carrier behind.

"Get her! Get her!" I heard someone call out.

A young black man ran out of the bus after the shooter. Two English tourists followed him.

I looked out the window. The plain woman was disappearing down the stairs to the subway.

Her pursuers were gaining on her.

I heard more shots and then the young black man threw out his arms and fell against the side of a newspaper kiosk.

It was strange. As he was falling I remembered a famous old photograph I had once seen in a museum, taken by a news photographer during the Spanish Civil War. A soldier who'd been hit by a bullet was falling, his arms thrown wide. This was exactly the same.

I had no idea what to do next. Other passengers were trying to help the three wounded people. I could tell that at least one of them was already dead.

Outside, a crowd gathered around the young pursuer who had been shot.

One passenger at the front of the bus was standing on his seat shouting incoherently. The bus driver was talking on his cell phone and trying to calm the man at the same time.

The window behind the seat where the victims had been sitting was smeary with blood.

I was astonished by my almost analytical calmness, although I knew quite well there would be repercussions once the initial shock wore off. I also had the fleeting idea that I was playing a part in a remake of the film *The Laughing Policeman*, which opens with a slaughter on a city bus.

Then I noticed the cat carrier still wedged in on the steps.

I retrieved it and brought it back to my seat, placing it on my lap. I sat there quietly.

The sirens were audible now—police cars, ambulances. They were coming closer and closer.

I could no longer see the gunshot victims. Passengers surrounded them. The circle of people was only a few feet from me, but I felt totally unconnected.

The cat meowed.

I opened the carrier. She was small and pitch black in color with a little bit of white mask.

There was a tag around her neck. It read in large print: HELLO! MY NAME IS TULIP.

I began to laugh; amidst all that carnage, I was laughing. Then I said to Tulip, "Hello! My name is Alice." And with that I closed the carrier.

Two EMS workers suddenly burst through the back door. They set about evaluating the damage to each victim and prepping them for the trip to the hospital.

One of the emergency people was a heavyset woman. She tried to revive the man lying in the aisle with mouth-to-mouth resuscitation, alternating with heart massage. But it was no use. He was dead.

She sat back on her haunches and caught sight of me.

"You look very calm," she commented, a bit resentfully.

"I am calm," I said. "I'm on my way to Eileen Fisher."

"Did you see it?"

"Yes."

"Was there an argument?"

"No."

"Did he say anything before he started shooting?"

"It wasn't a 'he.' "

She nodded. "Taking your cat to the vet?"

"No. I told you, I'm going to Eileen Fisher, on Ninth Street. I'm going to buy a coat."

The bus had by then filled up with police officers. They were escorting the passengers off.

The first blue uniform that approached me received the carrier in his arms.

"She isn't mine," I said as I pushed the box at him. "But her name is Tulip."

And then, as I was being escorted through the back door, the chickens came home to roost. My legs collapsed and my stomach became a Cuisinart chewing on steel wool.

Chapter 2

On the morning after the carnage, I went out at six-thirty to gather the papers. It was freezing.

Once back in the loft, I fed the cats, Bushy and Pancho, fed myself with coffee and heavily buttered toast, and then spread the papers out on the sofa to read about the bus shooting.

It became clear, however, that I was essentially reading my own description of the event . . . what I had told the police and the EMS workers.

There was a sketch of the shooter, obviously based on my attempt to revisualize that shy, plain face.

There was no mention of Tulip or the shopping bag.

Then I got to the meat, the sad, sorry meat of the articles—brief identification of the victims.

All the papers agreed that the dead were:

Calvin Rupp. The black man who had chased

the shooter toward the subway. A 31-year-old
law school student from Brooklyn. Single.

Victor Abado. Unemployed garment worker.
36 years old. Married. Two children. Manhattan resident.

Murray Price. 71-year-old retired schoolteacher. Widower. Queens resident.

The wounded person was Natasha Larish. 44-year-old accountant. Resident of Manhattan. Single.

I was mentioned as a valuable witness in all
the papers, but they all got my name wrong.
Lucy Nestleton, they called me.

This didn't really bother me. I like the name
Lucy.

The detective in charge of the investigation,
identified as Halleck, was quoted as saying that
the shooter's motive was unclear, though it was
logical that one of the victims was the original
target and the execution severely botched in that
"innocent" people also died.

What was missing from all the reports was, I
realized, the bus itself.

Hard to explain what I mean . . . what I was
thinking that morning . . . about the bus. I mean
the bus was primary. I had been spared injury,
true enough. Yet it was as if that vehicle was
sent into my life by some karmic force. Somehow it felt as if the tragedy of the shooting was
aimed directly at me. That's how I was thinking
at the time, a bit deranged.

I even, if I recall, chugged about the room like a doomed bus using that old Martha Graham technique.

The ringing phone interrupted me. It was Lester.

"Listen, Alice," he said. He always started off conversations like that, saying *Listen*. "Listen. I was reading the paper and they mentioned a Lucy Nestleton who witnessed a gruesome murder on a bus. And I suddenly got the funny feeling . . ."

"It was me, Les."

"My God. Are you okay?"

"I'm fine."

"Do you want to talk? Can we talk?" He often asked the little self-incriminating questions. I loved them. There was no need to answer. They were always accompanied by shrugs.

"Bring some croissants," I said.

He was there in twenty minutes with a bag of croissants from Taylor's, on Hudson Street. Had I known he was going there, I would have asked for muffins.

The minute he walked into my apartment, his face gave off one of those shocked signals that meant I wasn't looking very good, or rather I looked like a madwoman.

I tried to compose myself while making him coffee. He kept asking me questions about the shooting, and I kept shrugging them off or coming up with little quips.

He sat down on the sofa once the coffee was served. Bushy, my loquacious Maine coon, seemed not to like him. He moved away. Pancho, oddly enough, was interested. He stationed himself about three feet from Lester, on the arm at the other end of the sofa, and just stared at the stranger.

I was too agitated to sit . . . agitated by the newspaper stories and by the presence of Lester Rawls.

I paced back and forth in front of him. He had folded his long blue overcoat and placed it beside him on the sofa. He was wearing an old-fashioned ski sweater, a red one, with reindeer prancing across his chest.

He really did have a nice face. It was a bit too craggy, which was why he always played villains. And his nose was a little too prominent. And he had these eyes that looked every so often as if they were trying to escape from his head.

How can I say it? He looked like a hard-used, fifty-year-old man who still had a helluva lot of troubles and triumphs to come.

"Did it happen the way I read it?" he asked.

"Sure. If you believe a performance duplicates a script."

"I get your point."

I sat down suddenly next to him on the sofa.

I grabbed his knees with my hands so hard that he flinched.

"What's the matter?" he asked.

"Did you hear what I said?"

"Sure. That a performance can't duplicate a script."

"I'm talking nonsense, aren't I?"

"Maybe."

"Do you know what I really want to say?"

"No."

"I want to say something about Angela."

"Was there an Angela on the bus?"

"I don't know, Les. I'm talking about our Angela."

"*Our* Angela?"

"My character on *Mulberry Street*."

He didn't respond.

"Are you shocked that I'm talking about a role in a stupid TV series at a time like this?"

"Maybe."

"But don't you see? I did it all wrong. Remember how I prepared for the role?"

"Yes. I remember exactly, Alice. It was when we had coffee together the first time alone. You told me that a seventy-year-old woman who once functioned as a mob killer had to be schizoid. She always had to be operating on two levels."

"Exactly. On the one hand my Angela is

motherly. She makes people fell good. Warm. Wanted. But always there is something small and cryptic and violent about to burst through. As she is being motherly she also, without any drama, decapitates a spider with her foot."

"Right. I thought you were brilliant. Even if the spider decapitation was metaphorical. I think people are going to remember your character a long time after they've forgotten *Mulbery Street*."

"That's possible. But she's fake."

"Why?"

"Believe me, she's fake, Les. Don't you see what I did?"

"No."

"It's an acting class exercise. I conjured up my Angela. I constructed her out of books, movies, psychiatric articles. She's a pastiche. A piece of intriguing fluff."

"You're being harsh on yourself."

"No. Don't you understand? It was literary. Angela is a fiction. I got it all wrong. I produced a fake."

"Calm down, Alice."

"I did see Angela on the bus."

"What?"

"The shooter was Angela."

"But I thought she was a young woman."

"Yes. Of course. She was Angela as a young

woman. And there was none of that schizoid layering."

"What was there?"

"Nothing."

"There had to be something."

"There was calmness. There was a total lack of affect. There was simplicity. There was fluidity. But it was all like opening a jar. Do you understand what I'm saying? There was no complexity. There was a woman who took a gun out of a bag and—*Bang! Bang! Bang!*"

I pointed my finger at him, as if my hand were a weapon, and repeated: *"Bang! Bang! Bang!"*

He smiled nervously. "The paper reported that there were four shots on the bus."

"I said "bang" once more, very softly.

I got up and moved away from the sofa, a bit embarrassed by my theatrical rant.

"Is the coffee okay?"

"Excellent."

"You're lying, Les."

"Exaggerating."

"Is there a difference?" I pressed.

So then it happened. Look, like I said, we were getting closer and seeing each other more and more, and all we had done was kiss each other on the cheek upon arriving and going, and so suddenly after that idiotic conversation about my coffee he stood up and took a step toward me and I literally, to use the old cliché, rushed into his arms and we were kissing rather madly for our ages and we displaced a cat with a rush because we fell down on the sofa entwined.

It was only a moment later that I heard the dreaded sounds—clattering like stones flung against the loft windows.

I disentangled myself quickly, suddenly. I was frightened.

"What's the matter?" he asked.

I held up my hand for him to be quiet. He wouldn't understand my fear. Less than a year ago a young man had stood downstairs and flung pebbles at my window. He wanted to see me. He said he loved me. It was a child's crush. But he was murdered soon after that and for some reason I brought them together in my head—the murder and the pebbles.

The assault came gain. I walked to the window and stared down.

"It could be a drunk," Lester said. "Let me go downstairs and take care of it."

Again with my hand I cautioned him to be quiet and stay still.

I opened a window and leaned out. A cold blast of air almost blew me back . . . but I stuck my head out.

Believe it or not, it was Tony Basillio.

He had a bag of nuts in his hand and he was

casually throwing them upward in a sort of debauched Romeo and Juliet scene.

I shouted down: "What are you doing here? When did you get back?"

I could swear he was shivering. He was underdressed, wearing only a corduroy jacket and a muffler. It looked as if he'd put on weight.

"Buzz me in, Swede, and I'll reveal all," he shouted up.

Since I had just disentangled myself from a passionate embrace and the object of my passion was now seated calmly on the sofa, you might imagine that I would tell Tony, some other time.

But the sight of this man, whom I had known for many years and loved in some fashion so many ways, overwhelmed the temporary. I totally forgot about Lester Rawls in my confusion. And I buzzed Tony in.

He walked into the loft with a proprietary air, hissing good-naturedly at the cats. Bushy purred. Despite Tony's relentless teasing of him, Bushy loved Tony. Not crazy Pancho. He was off like a shot. At first sight of him, Pancho ran like hell and leaped up on the sink and then the top of the refrigerator where he crouched and glared.

Tony then kissed my hand, bowed, and said, "Swede, I have returned from Hades with gifts."

He handed me what looked like a half pound of coffee beans. Tony had never approved of my Medaglia d'Oro instant coffee.

Then he saw Lester.

"Who are you?" he asked.

I introduced them. Tony gave me a look that only a brazen philandering bastard of a hypocrite like him could have mastered. God knows how many starlets he chased in L.A. For if she was under twenty-five, lissome, and fey, Tony sprang. That was his M.O.

Lester shook hands with Tony, kissed me lightly on the cheek, and said, "I have to go."

He headed toward the door.

"Wait!" Tony ordered.

"What?"

"I've seen you before. You an actor?"

"Yes."

"You know how it is with us stage designers," Tony said, grinning. "There are only two kinds of actors—fat and skinny."

Lester made an attempt to smile.

"I got it! The Irish Arts Theater about five years ago. Right?"

"Right."

"It was a play about hunger strikers."

"That's it," Lester confirmed. "I played Bobby Sands."

"Damn!" Tony exclaimed.

Lester left. I sat down on the sofa. Tony stood in front of me.

"You miss me, Swede?"

"In my fashion."

"You look pale."

"Bad things have been happening."

"What? What? I thought everything was going good. I thought the first season on *Mulberry Street* was a wrap, and all you've got to do is wait for the money to start rolling in."

I was about to begin telling him about the bus slaughter. But the phone rang.

The voice on the other end was male and hard edged.

"Is this Alice Nestleton?"

"Yes."

"My name is Louis Nessem. I'm the acting director of RETRO. Can you come in and see me some time this week?"

"Pertaining to what?"

"I'd rather not say over the phone."

"You know," I blurted into the phone, "I used to work with RETRO. I mean, I was a consultant with you people."

"I am fully aware of your former connection with RETRO, Miss Nestleton. That is one of the reasons I am contacting you."

"I could be down there tomorrow morning, around ten. Are you still on Church Street?"

"No. We're on Beaver Street now. All the way downtown. Ten would be fine."

He gave me the new address and hung up.

Too many things were happening. I couldn't think. I didn't want to. Tony started to babble on about L.A. That was fine with me.

Chapter 3

I entered the building on Beaver Street that now housed RETRO with, as the poet says, fear and longing.

I had worked for RETRO briefly a few years ago. It was essentially a research and investigative unit set up and staffed by the NYPD to investigate important cold crimes, utilizing to a great extent the incredible information capacity of the then-new Criminal Investigation Database (CID).

They had hired me as a consultant to help in the investigation in a series of brutal unsolved murders of cat owners. It turned out to be a feline cult thing, something very sick. While there I was both respected and made fun of. I became known as the Cat Woman, and there were many bizarre caricatures of me pinned up on the bulletin board.

Then my contract expired and that was that.

There was no identifying name on the door of

the third floor, but RETRO was obviously much better funded now. There were a lot of offices and people and machines. The floor was heavily carpeted, but all the other furnishings were minimal. Absolutely nothing, it seemed, was allowed on the walls.

I was ushered into Louis Nessem's office. He was dressed in civilian clothes but his NYPD rank, from the sign on the desk, was captain. He was a portly man, dark complexioned, very bushy eyebrows, very little hair left on top, and dressed in tie, shirt, and suit that seemed much too small for him.

And I must admit, as he began to talk to me I had the sense that I was dealing with an honest, low-keyed man. That made me feel good.

He got very quickly to the point.

"I read the reports on that M8 bus shooting the other day. Your name rang a bell. So I went to our files and saw you had been on contract with us for a while. It was too good a coincidence to pass up."

"You lost me there, Captain Nessem," I said.

"My name is Louis. Call me that. Or call me Nessem. As for the coincidence—well, the shooter on the M8 gave you a cat to watch, didn't she? And how could she know that the beautiful blonde on the bus with her was the one known in legend as the RETRO Cat Woman?"

That irritated me. I snapped: "So you got me here to get my autograph?"

"Calm down, Miss Nestleton. I have no desire for your autograph, but I could use your help."

"On what?"

"On the relation between the shooting you witnessed on the M8 the other day and the shooting that didn't happen on an M14 three years ago."

"I have no idea what you're talking about."

"I'll tell you in a minute. But first . . . is it true you're in a big new crime series on TV?"

"It's a crime series. I'm in it. I have no idea how big it will be. It may last five episodes. That's what we've finished. They begin airing in March."

"RETRO does not discriminate against theater people. We have seven out-of-work actors on our computers."

"Are you offering me a job, Louis?"

"Yes. A short-term contract. Six weeks. Five thousand dollars and expenses. You work out of here."

"What do you want?"

"The Cat Woman sensibility, Miss Nestleton. I think you can make the connection."

"You mean between the two shootings?"

"Yes. Just listen. Three years ago a woman on an M14 bus in the morning, removed a weapon from a shopping bag and pointed it at fellow riders. No shots were fired. The gun either misfired or it was a toy. This shooter, who had no cat carrier with her like the woman on your M8 bus, dropped several cans of Sheba cat food as she was fleeing the bus."

"So?"

"So, the connections are powerful. In both cases it was a crosstown bus. In both cases it was morning. In both cases a woman in the back well removed a handgun from a shopping bag. In both cases there is a strong connection to felines."

"Which leads you to believe it is time for the Cat Woman to enter."

"I think you're beginning to make fun of me, Miss Nestleton."

"Call me Alice or call me Nestleton. And I'm not making fun of you. There's just a whole lot of history coming back."

"Well, this is a new RETRO. I need you here now because indeed you used to be called the Cat Woman. Because you see things in this area other people don't see. So, you go home and think on it and let me know some time today. Okay?"

"Fair enough."

We shook hands and that was that.

I walked out and headed north. Now I had a series that could make me rich and famous; a job offer at a place I had once loved; and two men who seemed to be desperate for me. Well, things were a bit out of control. I needed a consultation with Sam Tully.

Chapter 4

It was strange how I had grown apart from most of my friends except for the derelict mystery writer, old Sam Tully. That was exactly what I was thinking about as I trudged up the steps to his apartment on Spring Street.

As usual, his lunatic cat, Pickles, was on the window, begging to be let out onto the fire escape to proceed up to the roof for some pigeon hunting.

The apartment was freezing. Sam, grizzled and dressed as if he just left a retreat for alcoholic pickpockets, was sprawled on his "lounging" chair eating a cut-up banana with heavy cream.

As Sam always said, he could eat what he wished now because by all rights he should have been dead long ago from his drinking, smoking, and bad diet . . . so to attempt to preserve his life at this late stage would definitely cause it to end abruptly.

"Sit down, honey, and tell me what the hell

you're doing here. Am I correct that you are here to seduce me?"

"Hardly."

He pointed to his typewriter. "The machine is collapsing. Besides, no one seems to want to see Harry Bondo in print again. It's no great loss to humanity, but look at it from my standpoint."

Sam had had a brief success with a mystery series featuring a lunatic thug named Harry Bondo. He, Sam, had been trying to resurrect him and sell a new series by softening his hero around the edges. Alas, the publishers seemed to loathe Harry Bondo now, new or old.

"You ought to trim your beard and moustache, Sam."

"I ought to do a lot of things."

I sat down on what passed as his sofa. Pickles, still on the ledge, started to shriek for release. Sam threw a paperback book at him. Pickles dodged it easily and kept on screeching.

"Let him out," Sam ordered.

I went to the window, opened it, and let the beast out. He was gone in a flash. I shut the window and returned to the sofa.

"I'm listening," said Sam.

"I don't really want to bore you with my problems, Sam."

"I didn't know you had problems anymore. Hell, you're on a hit TV show. You got money in the bank."

"It's not a hit TV show. Not yet. We'll see."

He ignored my caution. "Yeah, Nestleton. I think we are both doing really good. I mean, you're affluent and I'm trying to write one long poem before I die. We both got sustenance. We both got a mission."

"Like Pickles?" I asked.

Sam laughed. "Yeah. Like Pickles, moving to the roof to get those pigeons."

Then I told him about Tony's return, about my situation with Lester Rawls, about the shooting incident on the bus, and about my interview with RETRO. I tried to reproduce Lou Nessem's exact words about the feline connections of the bus shootings.

"And all this is being revealed to me for what reason, Nestleton?"

"I don't really know, Sam. I guess I'm beginning to think you're wise."

"That is a delusion."

"No doubt. But my social circle has been shrinking."

Sam then closed his eyes and brought both hands to the side of his head in the mocking style of a person going into a trance. "Hold still, tall beautiful blond woman. Hold still. I am zeroing in on your aura or whatever the hell it is. Yes. Yes. It's coming. The answers are emerging."

And then he let out a big groan, lit a new

cigarette, and stated in a pontifical way: "Dump that sonofabitch Tony Basillio. Take Lester Rawls as your lover. Accept the job with RETRO." He clapped his hands. "I have spoken."

"Very funny."

"Only the dressing is meant to be funny, honey. I stand by my suggestions."

"How can I dump Tony?"

He laughed. "You always say that. About how long you and that Basillio have been together. But you never *are* together. I mean, he just came back, didn't he? Where has he been? Where is this togetherness you always talk about?"

"In the heart."

"You're starting to sound like a television actress."

"I'm not defending Tony. He has a lot of problems."

"The guy can't keep it in his pants."

"That's true."

"And he's a sponge. He has to be taken care of. You know what I mean. Damn, he's gotten all kinds of teaching jobs and theater jobs. They never last, do they?"

"Never."

"I never met this new guy of yours."

"You will."

"And you really like him?"

"Yes."

"So everything is settled. Right? You're gonna dump Tony, take up with this new guy for better or for worse, take the assignment with this RETRO, figure out what went down in both shootings, and then just wait for those residuals from *Mulberry Street.* Honey, I can see it now. You and this Rawls in Connecticut, on a small yacht, and me in a bar telling people how I knew her when she was the very soul of the committed Off-Broadway actor, incapable of vulgarity or triteness. And, I even knew her when she looked after cats for a living."

"The only trouble, Sam, is I need a reason to go back to RETRO, even on a temporary basis."

"You got plenty of reasons. You left in disgrace and now you're coming back in triumph. Right? I mean, in a way. And besides, you don't know anyone there anymore. And, deep down, when it comes to things criminal, you have a sick relationship to them. You like to roll in it, baby."

"How poetic of you, Sam."

"Did I dispense enough wisdom?"

"I think you did."

"Good. I'm getting weary."

"But there's something else happening."

"Honey, in this world there is always something else happening."

"I mean, I think I'm losing it, Sam."

"Losing what?"

"Talent maybe. Or skills. Or capacities. Call it what you want."

"You mean you can't act anymore? You mean the degradation of having a bit part in a cable series is just too much for the artistic Alice Nestleton?"

"I'm not talking about acting and I'm not talking about cat-sitting. I'm talking about what happened on the bus."

"Look, honey, the only thing I know about the bus shooting is what you told me."

"Well, let me tell you something else."

"I'm all ears," said Sam, grinning and lighting a new cigarette.

"I think I was the only person on the bus who interacted with the shooter."

"What about the people who got her bullets? Ain't that interaction, Nestleton?"

"Not funny, Sam. You know what I mean."

"No. I don't."

"Look. I think I was the only person on the bus who watched her, thought about her, even spoke to her on the bus."

"Okay."

"I even played one of my silly little games . . . you know . . . trying to figure out who she was . . . where she was going . . . what kind of life she led."

"Okay. So?"

"So, at no time did I ever get a sense of threat to me or anyone else."

"Why would you? The lady was cool."

"Sam, she had a gun in her bag. She was thinking death. She was there for death. A few years ago, no matter how cool she was . . . how filled with sangfroid . . . I would have picked something up."

"Maybe."

"Come on! Let's face it, Sam! There is a good possibility that I have lost that sixth sense one needs to have in a criminal investigation. In fact, the only thing I ever had going for me was that sixth sense."

"Too bad you never read the last Harry Bondo books."

"What do they have to do with what I'm talking about?"

"Well, there is this scene at the end of the book with Harry and his girlfriend, Masha."

"You mean Marsha?"

"No. Masha. And Masha tells Harry that she has this sixth sense that he is cheating on her. Do you know what Harry's response is?"

"Obviously I don't, because I didn't read the book."

"Harry says to her, 'A sixth sense is the last refuge of a malnourished idiot who is constantly depressed because he or she has only five toes on each foot.' "

Right there and then I called RETRO.

Nessem asked, "Don't you want a little more time to consider this?"

"No."

"Fine. You're on board. See you tomorrow morning."

Then I left Sam's Spring Street hovel and took a cab to the West Side, where Lester Rawls rented a large old apartment on a sublet.

We didn't say a word after he let me in. We went to bed and made love. Then we went out to eat, went to a Belgian movie at the Walter Reade, went for drinks, went back to his apartment and made love again, and then fell into an exhausted sleep.

They were beautiful hours. The problem was that large cloud hovering just above my head. Tony had to be told. Tony had to be told with firmness and gentleness that I was finally through with him.

I did it the next morning, on the way to my first official day at the new RETRO. It went badly, to say the least.

Chapter 5

I arrived at seven-thirty in the morning. Tony was fast asleep in what used to be my apartment on Twenty-sixth Street.

. He greeted me amorously. I pushed him away. He recovered and made me a cup of coffee. We sat at the small kitchen table and stared out the tiny window that fronted an alley.

"I'm glad you're here," he said.

"I'm glad I'm here," I agreed, though he didn't pick up my wryness. I was losing that ability I once had to articulate levels of sensibility with just a change of inflection. Age was taking it from me. Or maybe fatigue. Or maybe *Mulberry Street* had blasted it out forever . . . maybe it was good riddance to bad rubbish.

"Let's go out and have some breakfast. I missed those New York breakfasts."

"I can't, Tony. I'm expected somewhere."

"Come on, Swede. We have to get close again. Fast. You want to hear about L.A.? You want to hear some very funny stories?" He had this charming way of asking a question and running both hands through his still-thick black hair.

"That's the point exactly, Tony. Why I came here. We aren't going to get close anymore. We aren't close now. And the way things turned out, the whole script was a joke."

"What the hell are you talking about?"

"Us. It's over, Tony. And I mean over. And I mean surgically. The end. Kaput. I want no more of it."

He turned very pale and leaned his elbows on the table as if his body had become heavy.

"What are you talking about?" His voice was almost a whisper.

"Exactly what I said. I am dissolving the bonds. I don't know how many ways to say it. Surely you understand."

"This is a mistake, Swede."

"Maybe."

"You're confused. You're having problems. Maybe all this TV work is too much for you."

You know what I thought of at that moment. After he said those words? Well, I didn't actually think. I had a flashback. Not to some point in our past, some night of love or anything like that. No, I was back on the M8 bus and I was watching that very shy woman pull out a lethal weapon from her shopping bag and start firing.

And I wanted that weapon. And I wanted to

put a bullet in poor Tony's head the moment he said I was confused.

All I did was push my coffee cup away. But I did it so forcefully that the liquid sloshed out all over the table.

Then I stood up.

"So we know where we stand, Tony."

"I don't know anything. All I see is an hysterical lady."

"Don't call me. Don't write me. Don't come by. That's simple."

I headed for the door.

"Wait! Wait! You can't walk out on me like this," he shouted.

I opened the door and headed own the stairs. Tony followed me in his bathrobe, yelling.

"Twenty years, Swede. You just don't do something like this. I was thinking about you all the time in L.A. About how when I got back we were going to put all the nonsense behind us. We were going to be like we used to be. Don't you remember how it was, Swede?"

I walked out of the building without replying and caught a downtown bus almost immediately. To be honest, the moment he was out of sight I felt no anger, no remorse, no nothing. I knew I had to get to RETRO. I wanted to get there. I wanted to see Lester Rawls that evening. I was in total equilibrium . . . on a murder investigation. How right that old reprobate Sam Tully was!

Nessem of RETRO was all business when I arrived. He nodded his greeting and escorted me to a small cubicle which, I assumed, would be mine for the duration of the consulting project.

There was a metal desk and chair. On the desk was a slew of new office supplies—ballpoint pens, legal pads, boxes of paper clips. All for me.

Back on the desk was the PC.

Nessem said, "You can't access CID through the desktop. Okay? The CID room is at the end of the hall. You want any kind of information, any kind of search, just write your request on a sheet of paper and bring it over there. And you must send a duplicate of your request to me. Got it?"

"Yes."

He sat wearily on the only chair in the cubicle.

"Are you looking forward to this assignment?" he asked.

"Of course. Would I have taken the job otherwise?"

"I suppose not. But you do realize that we want you on the M14 shooting first, not the one you were involved with."

"I wasn't involved in the M8 shooting, Nessem. I witnessed it. I was traumatized by it. Besides, you're starting to confuse me. I thought there was no shooting on the M14. I thought the woman never fired a shot."

"She never did," he affirmed, "but because there is some reason to believe that she intended to fire her weapon—that it was a malfunction of the weapon that prevented discharge—that's why it was considered an attempted homicide."

"Makes sense."

"Right. And it also makes sense that you go talk to the Manhattan South homicide detective who worked the case originally. His name is Jeff Logan. Here's his number."

He slipped me a small piece of paper, scrap paper really. Like two kids in the back of the room passing dirty notes. That was something I had always liked about RETRO: It was a very high-tech place in which all personal relationships of any kind were conducted on the most primitive level.

Nessem left me alone in my cubicle. I pushed around my new supplies a bit, logged on to the PC, and then made my call to Detective Logan.

Logan agreed to meet with me—in an hour, in a café on Lispenard Street, just off Canal.

Then I phoned Lester. I told him where I was. We made small talk about new jobs. It was kind of amazing. I mean, we had made love for the

first time only last night. And we had been almost adolescent in our fumbling passion—desperate, cramped, wonderful. But here we were
talking nonsense as if nothing had happened . . .
as if we were coffee shop companions. Only at
the end of the brief conversation did the urgency
surface in a kind of desperate question from
him: "When will I be seeing you again?"

"Soon," I responded, and then went to meet
Logan, waving to my new co-workers as I exited
and wondering why Nessem hadn't introduced
me to them formally.

Detective Logan was already there, sitting in
front of a cup of coffee in the back of the café.
The lunch-hour crowd had not yet arrived, so
he was virtually alone.

I sat down across from him with a small orange juice and a straw. The café was pleasant,
with bookshelves along the walls for decoration.
There was a smell of greens and sun-dried to-
matoes in the air.

Logan seemed to be about thirty, with fading
red hair and a mournful thin face. He held his
cup between both hands and sipped. One of the
New York tabloids was in front of him, turned
to the sports pages.

"Are you with the department?" he asked.

"No. I'm just doing some consulting work
for RETRO."

He smiled, a bit sardonically, as if he had

dealt with flaky consultants in the past and knew exactly what to do.

"Well, how may I be of service?"

"I want to know about that M14 incident."

"You mean you want to make a connection with the M8 shooting."

"Don't you think there is a connection?"

"To be honest with you, lady, that whole M14 thing was a non-event."

"I don't understand."

"We couldn't even be sure that the object the woman held in her hand supposedly pointed toward her fellow riders was a gun. Understand? One woman on the bus reported the incident to the bus driver. He reported it to the police at the end of his run. That single woman passenger who reported the 'attempted homicide,' and who gave the driver the cans of cat food the 'shooter' allegedly dropped, is now dead. We were never able to find other passengers from that bus. Not a single person stepped forward to confirm the witness's story."

"Nothing else?"

"There really is nothing else. I think what happened was, a crazy bag lady got on the bus, walked down into the well of the bus and started waving a banana or something at the other riders and screaming, and one person believed it was a gun and after the crazy got off the bus she told the driver."

That was it. We sat together for a while, not saying a word. He drank his coffee. I drank my juice. I was suddenly so tired I could have wept. He left first. I put my head down on the table and fell asleep.

About twenty minutes later a busboy woke me by banging a cup on the table. I was quite embarrassed.

As I walked out, I realized I had been dreaming about that shy killer. And her question to me: "Are we close to the Broadway stop?"

Chapter 6

The next morning I left the house at six-thirty to buy the papers and treat myself to a good breakfast . . . something I don't usually do.

Nutrition was important now, wasn't it? I mean, I had a new job and a new lover.

I ignored the menu proffered in the Hudson Street Diner and ordered pancakes and sausages.

Then I relaxed and started to read the papers. The window near me was fogged over since it was freezing outside and warm inside. The food came very quickly and I devoured it, along with coffee and orange juice.

I had my coffee cup refilled and just sat there and watched the foggy window swirls. It was slowly becoming light outside. The window began to fill me with a kind of inchoate nostalgia. As a child I loved to trace designs on fogged windows. So I leaned over and wrote something on the window and felt foolish and silly but very happy.

But then I sat up very straight and felt like an utter idiot because I saw what I had written on the fogged window in my cramped hand: "Hello. My name is Tulip."

I quickly erased it with my hand, paid the bill, and headed home.

As I turned the last corner toward my loft, Tony Basillio stepped out from a storefront and directly into my path.

I stopped.

"What are you doing here?" I asked him, so startled by his sudden appearance that for a moment I nearly let out a scream for help.

He held out his hands in innocence. "I am doing nothing," he said, and he stepped aside a bit. I started to hurry past him.

But what he said to me stopped me and infuriated me: "I understand now, Swede," still using that stupid appellation for me even though I had told him eight million times I was not Scandinavian and didn't like the nickname.

"What do you understand, Tony?"

"I didn't know what you were going through. I didn't know what had happened to you. I mean the shooting. I mean the dead people. I mean I just didn't know."

"Now you do."

"Sure, you'd be mad at me. I wasn't around when you needed me. But now that's all over, Alice Nestleton. I will not leave again. I will be around every time you look up . . . like that playwright said . . . in pain and in love."

"You're going to be nowhere for me, Tony. What I told you is the truth. It's over."

"No. Listen, Alice. Let me move in. Let's just try it. Let's just be quiet and together for a few weeks and see what it's like."

"No."

He pointed a finger at me. "You're sleeping with that guy, aren't you? The guy I met at your loft."

I didn't respond. I proceeded with my journey. He followed just behind me and a bit to the right.

"Okay. Okay. Look. Who gives a damn? Sleep with who you want, Swede. Sleep and be happy. But we can still be together. We can still be together. I miss you. I missed you so much in California I used to wander around trying to find animal shelters so I could look at cats that reminded me of Bushy and Pancho."

I wasn't going to respond anymore. I wasn't going to listen. I reached my door and opened it. We both sort of paused. We were both sort of frozen between the door and the street.

"We can try it, Swede," he pleaded. Oh, when Tony Basillio started to plead with his sad Mediterranean eyes, it was very hard to withstand. And there was a bitter cold wind swirling around us.

But I would not, could not, be swayed. I slipped through the door and shut it quickly behind me. He was left outside, where I wanted him. I leaned against the door and tried to sense what he was doing, what he would do next.

Would he beat against the door?

Would he park himself there and wait for me to emerge again? Would he phone? Would he rant or cry or God knows what?

I heard nothing. I had no idea what he was doing. Or where he was going.

Slowly I walked upstairs, showered, and dressed. It was still too early to leave for RETRO. I made myself another cup of coffee.

Bushy jumped up on my lap and started snuggling. I said to him: "Hello. My name is Tulip."

Pancho began to make furious runs around us in wider and wider circles being chased, as usual, by his own extensive cast of nonexistent enemies. For all I knew, one of them might have been Tulip.

I wanted to call Lester.

Instead I turned on the radio. A news station was reporting how the pattern of the traffic lights on a certain street in the borough of Queens was being adjusted to protect pedestrians. Too many of them, it seemed, were dying trying to cross the street.

For some reason I found that hilarious. I burst out laughing with such force that Bushy leapt off me and fled.

Keep laughing, you fool, keep laughing, I muttered to myself. And I did. But then I had to get to work. The Cat Woman is rarely late.

Chapter 7

When I arrived at RETRO that morning, after the unfortunate meeting with Tony and a rather substantial breakfast, I was feeling a bit queasy.

My stomach settled quite nicely when I began to read the memo Louis Nessem had prepared for me, which was taped to the computer monitor.

His memos were wonderful. They were simply statements, one after another.

And this one was keeping me informed as to the case or cases.

To: Nestleton
From: Nessem
Re: M8 shooting et al

- Weapon has been identified as a .25 caliber handgun; uncommon weapon.
- Prints possibly belonging to shooter found in bus but not in system; no I.D. yet; description (very tentative) from now de-

ceased witness on M14 is of a much older woman and bears no resemblance to M8 shooter.

- Different shooters do not lessen connection in my estimation.
- Detective Halleck working the M8 murders has been informed of you and your interest; please contact him.
- Cat and carrier left on bus have been lost/ misplaced by crime scene people and/or ASPCA. We are following up.

And that was that. I was placing the memo in the top drawer of my desk when Nessem entered the cubicle.

"You read it?" he asked.

"Yes," I replied, deciding not to talk about my vexation at the misplacement of Tulip.

"Did you speak to Logan?"

"Yes."

"And?"

"He's skeptical."

"About what?"

"About whether the M14 was an attempted homicide and whether it has any relation to the M8 murders."

Nessem made an abrupt movement with his hand, as if Logan's skepticism were worthless.

Then he gave me a most peculiar look. I didn't know what that look signified, but it made me uneasy all the same. That is, I didn't know until he leaned against my desk, and in an almost astonishing display of intimacy said: "I want to hear from the center of you."

"What?"

"You know what I mean. That's why you're here, Miss Nestleton."

"My center, Captain Nessem? You talk like one of those philosophical potters. But you're not wearing a smock."

"Don't get cute with me. I don't need it and I don't deserve it."

"Then say what you mean to say."

"I'm talking about the cat thing."

"Aah."

"I want to know what you feel about the connection."

"You mean between the missing M8 cat, Tulip, and the cat food from M14?"

"Yes, yes, of course. I mean, sure, it is very early . . . but do you have a sense of something . . . an intuition, no matter how vague it is?"

"You mean something feline that illuminates all the carnage."

"Beautifully put, Nestleton. Beautifully put. That's exactly what I mean."

"I'm afraid I have nothing for you at this time."

Nessem gave me a crooked smile and left. I called Detective Halleck.

*   *   *

My meeting with the lead detective in the M8 murder investigation, Karl Halleck, took place in his unmarked vehicle that afternoon. He sat in the driver's seat and I sat beside him in the passenger seat.

The vehicle was parked, for some reason, in front of a new dress boutique on Mott Street, west of Canal.

The engine was running and the vehicle was in neutral.

I remembered his horselike face, vaguely, from a few hours after the shooting.

He was a big man and his body seemed to have to curve into itself to fit into the driver's seat and behind the wheel. After I slid in and introduced myself, he stared at my legs and lap in a rather vulgar fashion—but I did not react.

The situation was very awkward. I mean, I was there, essentially, because Nessem wanted me to be there. But he, Nessem, had just given me a memo on the status of the M8 Case, most of which probably came from Halleck, so why did Nessem want me to see Halleck? Probably to just touch base, to make contact, to provide a conduit.

I really had nothing to ask Halleck at that time. Besides, I was a witness to the murders and Halleck the investigator. Since when do witnesses interview detectives assigned to the case?

Well, all these things conspired to make it a very awkward situation, but I really had nothing to worry about, because Halleck resolved everything with a kind of nastiness.

He said: "Look. Let me put my cards on the table. I know who you are, lady, where you come from, who you're working for, and why. I will help you in any way I can. I will answer all your questions. I will give you what you need when you need it. But be clear about something: To me, RETRO is a glory-seeking pimple that should be squeezed out of the NYPD. It sniffs out current cases that it thinks will make it look like cold cases are being revived. It's the most bullshit operation I have ever seen in my life. So there it is. You know where I stand. But, like I said, ask any question you want. I'll answer them for you. I'm here for you."

"How could you lose a cat and a carrier during a murder investigation?" was my reply.

Then I got out.

"Wait!" he ordered.

I kept the door open and looked in from outside.

"Yes?"

"Did Nessem tell you about the cat? That it's missing?"

"Yes."

"Something else is missing."

"What?"

"Get back in for a minute."

I followed his orders.

"In your original statement you mentioned that the shooter was also carrying a shopping bag."

"That's right."

"Well, that's missing, too."

"Are you serious?"

"Yeah."

I was astonished. I said: "The cat is one thing. I mean it seems to have been misplaced in transit. But the shopping bag was evidence. I mean, the woman took the gun out of her shopping bag."

"So you said," he replied nastily.

"Do you think I was lying about that?"

He didn't answer that question. He said: "We think the shopping bag fell out of the back door of the bus either during the shooting or after she fled. We found a few pieces of a shopping bag. It was pretty ripped up."

"Was there writing on the bag that identified it as coming from the Metropolitan Museum of Art Gift Shop?"

"Yes. And we also found a small bottle of cheap perfume, gift-wrapped. Do you remember seeing something like that in the bag?"

"I saw a whole bunch of gifts in her shopping bag. Small ones. All gift-wrapped. Like Christmas wrapping. I thought they were belated

Christmas gifts. They could have been perfume.
I just don't know."

"Well, we traced the perfume. It was bought
in one of those cut-rate perfume stores on East
17th Street. The clerk couldn't give us a description, but she remembered that the woman customer had bought several bottles in early
December and had paid cash. So maybe they
were Christmas presents the shooter never
delivered."

"Are you sure it was the shooter's perfume?"

"No!" he snapped. "But it was lying just beside the bus and close to the ripped-up bag."

"What do you think happened to the rest of
the gift-wrapped packages?"

"Probably people walking by picked them up.
Free gifts. Just lying there. Hell, I would have
picked one up."

There was silence. The man made me feel
uncomfortable.

"Anything else, Detective?"

"Yeah. The gun."

"What about it?"

"In your statement you said you saw the
woman pull the gun out of the shopping bag."

"That's what I saw."

"So you said. But obviously the lady wasn't
walking around with the weapon on top of the
packages, or you would have seen it, right?"

"I don't know what you're getting at."

"Didn't she have to go deep into the bag to get the gun?"

"I never saw her *dig* into the bag. I just saw her remove the gun."

"Easily?"

"Yes. She didn't seem to root around in the bag to find it. She just pulled the weapon out."

"Is this line of questioning bothering you?"

"No."

"You sound irritated. Hell, you're a hotshot consultant for RETRO—you ought to take it in stride."

I got out of the car and slammed the door shut.

As I walked away, he rolled down the window and shouted out: "Is it true they call you the Cat Woman?"

Chapter 8

I woke up, and for a moment I didn't know where I was. Then I saw a man in my bed. But I didn't know his face. I turned over and started to rise, as if to flee the bed, and then I looked up at the very high ceiling. After that, I settled down.

I knew exactly where I was and who I was with.

The man beside me was Lester Rawls. We were in his subleased apartment on 100th Street and West End Avenue.

It was four o'clock in the morning. I slipped out of bed and walked into the living room. His windows looked onto the Hudson River and across to Jersey.

I was starting to feel peculiar about this new affair with Lester, as I was getting deeper and deeper into it. Peculiar is a bad word. Let's say I was searching for the residuals. This was the second time I had made love with him, the first time I had spent the night. And everything was fine . . . except before and after the sex, when there was really very little at all. The passion did not transcend the bed. And that made me a little nervous.

There was a moon, and the river was illuminated. The Hudson tide was moving fast toward the mouth of the bay.

"Are you okay?"

I turned suddenly to the words. It was Lester. He had a towel around his waist. I was absolutely naked.

"Did you ever play a role naked?" he asked.

"Not that I recall."

"I would find it difficult," he admitted.

"You look very good for your age," I noted.

"You too."

"Your body is your mike," I said, throwing out that old acting school saw.

"The variant I heard is, Your body is your megaphone."

"What about—Your body is your doom."

"Never heard that one."

I laughed. I had made that one up. I looked back at the river. One could tell that it was brutally cold out and the wind was whipping the water. But his apartment was as warm as toast, even at four in the morning, even with the frigid air banging at the windows.

We were both silent for a long time.

"My brother called me yesterday," Lester said. "You know he still lives on the Cape. I told him about you. He's very anxious to meet you."

"And I, him," I replied politely.

"Maybe we can go up and see him next week," he suggested.

"Sure."

"I feel very good, Alice. I don't remember ever feeling so good, at least not in a whole bunch of years. But I knew this was going to happen between us. I knew it from the first moment we were introduced to each other on the set. At the read-through. Remember?"

"Of course I remember. But I thought you were taken with me only because you like tall women."

He laughed.

"But what happens, Les, if you meet a seven-foot Rumanian lady?"

"Then I dump you."

Then he came over to me and we stared at the river together. Then we went back to bed and made love again.

I got home at ten in the morning.

My felines were enraged at my tardiness in feeding them breakfast. They snarled and complained as I prepared their dishes.

As they ate I checked the phone messages. There was only one: Sam wanted me to have lunch with him in Soho.

I knew exactly what he meant by lunch in Soho. We would meet at Dean & Deluca on Prince and Broadway; it was a fancy, overpriced gourmet shop. Sam would purchase a pound of potato salad and we would share it at the coffee counter. Then we would go into a bar, Fannelli's, two blocks west, and have some drinks. That was Sam Tully's typical Soho lunch. He had other kinds of lunches that were much less high-toned and the bars and bodegas much rougher.

I did go meet him, and by twelve-thirty we were comfortably ensconced at Fannelli's among the tourists and the old alcoholic painters. The potato salad lunch in the gourmet shop had been less than perfect because it was one of those rare times that a sprig of parsley was not in the potato salad and this upset Sam greatly.

Now at Fannelli's he was drinking Bass Ale and smoking Newports, the smell of which often sickened me, but not during that lunch.

I was drinking club soda with a piece of lime.

"So what's up at RETRO, Nestleton?" Sam asked.

"You wouldn't believe it."

"Try me."

"The head of it, Nessem, thinks I'm some kind

of mystic or psychic. He asked me if I had any theories yet. You know what I mean . . . cat-related theories . . . feline constructions . . . bizarre occult entanglements based on Egyptian cat god worship that ties together two disparate shootings on two different bus lines even though one wasn't even a shooting."

"Did he really use language like that, honey?"

"No, Sam. Of course not. He'd be too embarrassed. But that was what he wanted to say."

Sam grunted in amusement. He started drinking whiskey in addition to his ale and I saw him pay the bartender in crisp new fifties. Tully seemed to alternate between extreme poverty and sudden fleeting wealth. I never understood where he got the infusions of cash; his books were no longer being published and he didn't get Social Security because he had never paid into the system.

I graduated up to ginger ale with lemon. The bar was getting more and more crowded but we were secure at the front two seats, with a lovely window looking out on Prince Street.

Sam and I were silent for a while, listening to a tourist couple arguing about the food . . . about the chili in particular.

Then Sam blew some Newport smoke into my face and as I was gently choking, said, "Honey, it's about time you told me. I've been letting you slide long enough."

"Told you what?"

"About the shooting."

"I told you already, Sam."

"No, you didn't. I mean, you gave me report-age. I want to know what you experienced, Nestleton."

"Oh, for heaven's sake. You're starting to sound like an old method-acting teacher."

"Humor me."

"It's difficult to explain. I mean, sometimes when I think back on it I see myself being really calm and clear-headed, almost as though I was merely an observer watching a film. And some-times I get a sudden stab of—guilt, I suppose. The feeling that I participated . . . even that I enabled the killer because I was the only one on the bus she spoke to . . . I was the one she asked directions."

"I'm getting confused here. You think you had something to do with this horror?"

"I'm confused myself, Sam. And to boot, the NYPD lost or misplaced the cat. And there I am . . . Cat Woman . . . without a cat."

"Anything on the victims?"

"Nothing yet. That's the only place . . . the only way we'll get a leg up here. You agree?"

"Probably. If the shooter was aiming for one of them."

"You mean you think it possible she was

shooting randomly? No, Sam. If you saw her you wouldn't say that. Believe me."

Suddenly I saw the blood drain from Sam's florid face.

"What's the matter?" I asked urgently, bending over and grabbing his arm.

"We got trouble," he said.

He jerked his head toward the window.

I looked. What I saw was incredible.

Tony Basillio was outside the window of the bar, pressing his face against the glass and making grotesque faces at us as if he were a kid.

"He's drunk," Sam declared.

"And he's in pain," I added.

I started to head outside. Sam grabbed me. "Uh-uh, honey. You don't want to go out there."

I sat back down on the barstool.

"Ignore him," Sam counseled.

I did so, and when I turned back, about two minutes later, he was gone. I was too sad to talk anymore.

We sat in silence for a long time. Sam kept smoking and drinking and humming. I kept getting more and more depressed and agitated about Basillio in the window.

Finally I blurted out: "If he becomes psychotic, it's my fault."

"Did you really tell him it's all over? Did you really make it clear?"

"Yes."

"Then I guess you're right, honey. I guess you maybe just did send him around the bend."

I couldn't tell whether Sam was joking or not. I asked him: "Were you sure he was just drunk?"

"No one is just drunk."

"Do you think he would try to hurt me, Sam?"

My question seemed to make Sam very uncomfortable.

He said: "Look, Nestleton, you know your friend and I don't get along. We never did."

"Do you know why?"

"Probably for the same reason you finally dumped him."

"Which is?"

"You're asking *me*?"

"I'm sick of him, Sam."

"Okay."

"It was just the sum total of everything he did and didn't do."

"Okay."

"Year after year . . . it was only getting worse."

I kept throwing quick glances at the window to see if Tony had returned. He hadn't.

"Come to think of it," Sam said, "I never saw you two looking like lovers in the grand tradition. You know, flowers, champagne, ecstasy. No, I always got the sense of army."

"Army? What are you talking about?"

"Like you were two soldiers slogging along a muddy road to a battle."

"That's depressing, Sam."

"Sorry. But remember, I haven't known you and him that long. Maybe it was better before I came on the scene."

"Much better. Believe me."

"Where did you meet Tony?"

"In acting school. When I first came to New York. He was in several of my classes at the Dramatic Workshop."

"Love at first sight, honey?"

"Hardly. He was obnoxious, wisecracking, and disruptive in class. I thought he was a good-looking idiot. And he thought I was Daisy Mae who had come to the big city fresh off the farm to sing songs from *Oklahoma*."

"I didn't know you sang."

"I didn't. Then or now. Anyway, all the students at the Workshop used to hang out at a bar on Tenth Avenue. Sooner or later, I realized he wasn't as obnoxious as he seemed to be. And he realized I wasn't as unhip as he thought. And that's when it started."

I ordered a Bass Ale. The place had gotten very crowded. I found myself pushed even closer to the window Tony had stared into.

"That first time we were together—it didn't last long," I admitted.

"A week?"

"No. Almost three months. But they were good months."

"I'm sure they were, honey. To a girl from the Minnesota woods, Tony must have been exotic as hell."

"Like a bird of paradise," I admitted.

I sat up very straight. I stared at myself in the mirror. I could see Sam also; he was looking at me with concern. Did he think Tony was dangerous now? Did he think I was dangerous to myself?

"And then what happened?" he asked.

"I don't remember exactly. But it ended with a fight. And he left the class. And then I met someone else and got married. Did you know I was married once, Sam?"

"Yeah, you told me."

"It didn't last long."

"When did you run into Tony again?"

"Oh, that's a long crazy story."

"I've got nothing but time."

"Well, a whole lot of years went by. I heard stories about him. I heard that he had given up acting for stage design. I heard that he was getting a reputation for wild sets. I heard that he had won an award for a *King Lear* production at Lincoln Center. And then I heard nothing. In a sense I forgot all about him."

"Until when?"

"About ten years ago. And this is the crazy part. I had to Xerox a script so I went into one of those copying stores in the East Village. It was part of a chain called Mother Courage. I got into an argument with the clerk because he did a very sloppy job and didn't apologize or offer to do it over again."

"The clerk was Tony?"

"No, no. But the argument heated up and the boss, the owner of the chain who just happened to be in that store at that time, ran out to see what the yelling was all about. The boss was Tony Basillio. It seemed he had given up on the theater, married, had kids, moved to New Jersey, and started a copier business."

"And then what happened?"

"The obvious, Sam. The obvious. We started up again."

"Right away?"

"I think that same afternoon. It was not as good as the first time, but almost. We stayed together. He decided to leave his wife and kids. He sold the business and gave them the money. Then he threw himself back into the theater. And we lived happily ever after."

"You want another beer?"

"No."

"You want to leave?"

"Not yet."

"If he starts following you around, Nestleton, call the cops. Don't take any chances."

"Okay. Any other suggestions?" My tone was a bit mean. It was unwarranted.

"Yeah. Don't sit in bars with old men. It induces nostalgia. And you know what Harry Bondo says about nostalgia."

"I forget."

"So do I, but it ain't good."

Chapter 9

There was no memo waiting for me when I arrived at RETRO the next morning. Captain Nessem was. And the usually dour man was positively glowing.

He was not alone. A tall, very conservatively dressed black woman was beside him, her hands folded. He introduced me to Millie Lorca, director of RETRO's field operations.

"Are you related to the poet?" I asked.

"No."

Nessem said, "We found the cat."

"That's wonderful!" I exclaimed.

Millie Lorca took something out of her pocket and handed it to me. My God! It was the tag that was around the cat's neck. HELLO. MY NAME IS TULIP.

"Where is she?"

"At an animal shelter in Queens," Nessem admitted.

"How did she get there?"

"We haven't the slightest idea. It was just one of those foul-ups that happened during intense investigations. I mean, the EMS people were treating the wounded and dying. The cops were trying to get witnesses. You gave the cat in the carrier to someone you can't identify. That someone must have left it alone for a minute. Or just forgot about it. And someone picked it up and took it to a shelter. The problem is, while the shelter has the cat, the carrier is gone. There is not a trace of it."

"That's too bad," I noted. "You can pick up a lot of information from a carrier."

"Like what?" Millie Lorca asked, being a bit patronizing.

"Well, why don't I start with the obvious," I snapped, looking at her sternly. "For one, some people write their name and address somewhere on the carrier—like a luggage tag. Or they keep emergency vet information taped to a wall or the handle . . . the name and address of the cat's vet . . . the phone number of the closest animal hospital. Things like that."

She didn't reply. Nessem took the TULIP tag from me and swung it like a bell.

"I'd like you to get out there quick," he said to me.

"I'm on my way."

I left the RETRO office immediately, took the

train uptown and then the bus across the 59th Street Bridge into Sunnyside, Queens.

To be honest, there was a brief hiatus between the train and the bus.

I went into Bloomingdale's for about a half hour. It wasn't really a shopping expedition; I didn't buy anything. It was simply a little nostalgia because when I first came to New York as a young actress I virtually lived on the main floor of Bloomingdale's, fascinated in a morbid way with the spectacular perfume department and traversing from one side to another to get my wrist sprayed with free whiffs of the scents from eager salesgirls.

Once I crossed the bridge into Sunnyside, I was all business. The shelter was under the shadow of the El. It was obviously a nonprofit community operation with dedicated volunteers tending to a battered battalion of beasts rescued from the streets.

They were waiting for me, obviously proud that one of their guests had been part of a flamboyant crime.

Tulip was in her own cage, lying down on her side next to the feed bowl, one of her paws just outside the cage. She looked reflective, perhaps remorseful.

I was left alone with the witness.

I tugged gently at her exposed paw. She gave me a dirty look.

"Remember me, Tulip?"

I don't think she did. She stared once more, hard, and then turned away.

She was exactly the way I had seen her on the bus, or remembered seeing her—small, black, white mask, well formed.

I opened the cage and lifted Tulip out, holding her against and over my shoulder. She seemed quite content.

"I guess jail ain't so bad after all, Miss Tulip," I murmured.

She was, I realized, younger than I thought. Maybe two or three years old. And she was more powerfully built than I had thought . . . her frame was very strong and lithe under the short-hair coat.

I circled the room and let her know what kind of information I needed:

Her relationship to the shooter.

How long she had lived with the shooter.

Whether the shooter had planned the carnage.

Where the shooter had gotten the weapon.

Whether there were any other pets at home.

Whether the shooter deliberately abandoned her on the bus.

Why she was called Tulip.

Where the shooter had obtained her.

Who groomed her and who did her nails.

She told me nothing and I intuited nothing

from her. I placed her back in the cage, noticing that there was no dry food at all.

So Tulip ate only canned food? Cheap or expensive? Maybe only the kind of food that was in the cans that accompanied the woman on the M14 . . . the woman who had brought no cat, fired no weapon, and left only Sheba cat food tins.

Tulip curled up in the back of the cage and ignored me.

I walked outside the cage room into the small sitting area, now filled with shelter volunteers. They seemed to know about their celebrity cat, abandoned by a murderess on a city bus. They tried to help me with theories. They tried to recall every moment of the cat's life since she entered the shelter. None of them had any idea where the carrier was or who had delivered the cat to the shelter.

Tulip, I also learned, was a silent cat. She had never hissed or meowed since arriving at the shelter. Occasionally she rumbled low in her throat and stomach, which might have signified contentment, but no one was sure.

She did not seem at all interested in the other guests at the shelter. Dog, cat, or reptile.

I went back into the cage room and stared at Tulip for a long time.

It was obvious to me that my vaunted feline intuition was not functioning.

The Cat Woman was a bust.

I thanked my shelter hosts and headed back to RETRO, totally avoiding Bloomingdale's.

Back at RETO by noon, I worked relentlessly until four, doing absolutely nothing but putting away all my office supplies and trying to understand the administrative and personnel complexities of RETRO.

I would have gone home then if a very happy Millie Lorca had not materialized and invited me to come quickly to the CID room . . . the holy of holies . . . the home of the criminal investigation database, a room filled with computers, printers, and machines I couldn't even identify.

She led me to a small conference area that was situated in the back of the computer room.

Nessem sat at one end of the table with several sheets of paper in his hand. On the table in front of him was a small recording device.

Seated next to him was one of the gurus of the place—a man named Wallace who always wore a kind of scarf, as if he was perpetually cold.

Millie Lorca sat down and motioned that I should do the same.

"Did you see the cat?" Nessem asked.

"Yes. I was there for several hours."

"And?"

"Well . . . there's not much I can say right

now. Except the cat is in good health given its adventures."

"I'm looking forward to your report," he said.

"Of course. As soon as I can."

Then he leaned forward and activated the recording machine, speaking the date and time into it, rewinding to test the sound, then sitting back.

He held up the sheafs of paper.

"CID has made a significant breakthrough which might provide motive for the M8 shooting."

Nessem gestured to Wallace.

Wallace said: "One of the victims on the bus, if you recall, was a seventy-year-old retired teacher named Murray Price. Mr. Price was a Queens resident and a widower. His wife, Hannah Klein Price, died a year ago. But Mr. Price was married before that. The first wife was Carla Bonfiglio Price. She died too."

"Talk a little slower," Nessem said, gesturing to the recording machine.

Wallace nodded assent, then continued. "This is the background. What we found in State of California records is simple fact. Murray Price was a witness in a court case about two years before he married Carla Bonfiglio. In fact, the case involved his future wife, who had been indicted with several individuals on fraud and extortion charges. All of them, including Price,

worked for a large and successful placement
agency that specialized in advertising and PR
personnel. Bonfiglio pleaded out and testified
against her fellow workers, and Price confirmed
her testimony. Price, of course, had not been
charged at all, although he worked there."

Wallace shut up and just grinned at us. It was
an incredible excavation obviously made possible by the fact that the database now included
all names in state court cases over time. The
trouble was you had to know where to look. It
would not occur to the average homicide detective in New York to search California court records more than a decade past and if he did
check, he might have limited his search to in-
dictees and not have gone off on another, more
obscure path—witnesses.

Yes, the whole thing was heady. A hundred
new investigative paths seemed to be open to
us now. But we were all brought down to earth
a little by Millie Lorca, who said, "So?"

Nessem spoke sharply. "So Bonfiglio's testimony, with the help of Price, sent two men to
jail for a long time."

"Of course," Lorca said. 'I'm sorry. I wasn't
thinking. Revenge. Maybe a child or a wife or
a sister."

"If the primary target on the bus was Price,
most definitely it could be payback for that
conviction."

There was a long period of silence as if we were all in awe of our success.

Nessem said: "What has to be done next is clear. Get the transcripts of the California case. I'm sure the detectives working the bus shootings will have no trouble obtaining them."

Then he leaned over, turned off the recorder, and removed the tape.

He held it up to the light for a moment as if he could spot an imperfection in the transmission, and then slid it across the conference table to Lorca, saying, "Make a dupe and get it to Detective Halleck, please."

He looked at me. "When can I expect that Tulip report?"

Not knowing what to say, I said, "Tomorrow."

"Good," he replied. "There's something else you should do, Nestleton. Halleck is interviewing Natasha Larish tomorrow in St. Vincent's."

For a moment I didn't know the name. Then I remembered. She was the person who survived the attack. I remembered the newspaper report. Single. Resident of Manhattan. Accountant.

Nessem elaborated: "She was shot through the right shoulder and the bullet spiraled down and came out her thigh. Awful bloody, but not fatal. I'd like you to monitor the interview."

"Of course," I agreed.

"It's scheduled for eleven in the morning."

And then the meeting was adjourned. I went home and began to write the first draft of my report on my "interrogation" of Tulip. It got crazier and crazier and I kept ripping up the pages. I couldn't even think of anything to make up. So eventually all I did was give a detailed description of the shelter, the cat, and the staff.

At the end of this brief report I used a phrase that I hoped would mollify Nessem's yearning for my Cat Woman wisdom.

I wrote:

Important note. There were many philosophical/criminological aspects to Tulip's reactions. I will explore them in future reports.

As Tony Basillio might say, *Oh, brother!* Alice, I thought, you are full of it.

St. Vincent's Hospital. Eleven a.m. I met Detective Halleck outside the room. He was unfriendly but correct. We both understood now that I was being used by Nessem as a representative of RETRO, an observer, without any power to alter Halleck's behavior, investigative or otherwise. I was not happy to be there. This was wasting time. Nessem had charged me with investigating the old case, the M14 shooting, and tying it to the M8 one. I should be interviewing the bus driver on the M14 that day, not monitoring the questioning of Natasha Larish.

Natasha was propped up in bed. She was a stout woman with a thick, kindly face and a great deal of light brown hair flaring out. The nurse who was combing her hair left abruptly when we entered. Natasha looked pale and weak. Her dressings had obviously just been changed.

Halleck introduced us; it was clear she did not recognize me from the bus.

Halleck pulled up a chair beside the bed and placed a cassette recorder on the end table. I stood several feet behind him.

Here is what I heard:

HALLECK: This won't take long, Miss Larish. But we need some information.

LARISH: I'll do what I can.

HALLECK: (taking a drawing of the inside of the bus and showing it to her) Can you show me exactly where you were seated?

LARISH: (pointing to a spot) There.

HALLECK: (marking the spot with a ballpoint pen and putting the drawing aside) Why were you on that bus at that time, Miss Larish?

LARISH: I was going to meet a friend of mine at a coffee shop on Second Avenue. Then we were going to K-mart.

HALLECK: In other words, you were planning to get off at Second Avenue.

LARISH: Right.

HALLECK: Where did you get on the bus?

LARISH: Seventh Avenue.

HALLECK: Did you see the shooter when you got on?

LARISH: I'm not sure. I did notice a young woman with a cat carrier, but I don't know when I noticed her.

HALLECK: Well, we think she got on the same stop as you.

LARISH: That's possible. I just don't know. A lot of people got on at Seventh.

HALLECK: When you did notice her, did she seem familiar?

LARISH: No.

HALLECK: Did she look at you?

LARISH: I don't think so.

HALLECK: (taking out the police sketch that was drawn with my input and showing it to her) Could you study this for a minute?

LARISH: Okay. (takes the sketch and looks at it; then hands it back)

HALLECK: Is it an accurate representation of the shooter?

LARISH: Not really.

HALLECK: Why not?

LARISH: She was a little heavier. And her hair was a little longer. Also, the eyes are not right. They were narrower . . . more Asian.

HALLECK: Are you saying the woman was Asian?

LARISH: No. No. I'm just saying the eyes.

HALLECK: Were you looking at her when she pointed the weapon?

LARISH: I did see her and the gun for just a second. Before I heard the shots. But it was very fast. I noticed something funny about the back door. That's all. And then suddenly it was happening. I saw her, heard shots, felt this incredible pain. All of it seemed to happen at once.

HALLECK: Have you ever been hurt on a bus before?

LARISH: Once. A couple of years ago I was on a bus that stopped short and several passengers got hurt. Not bad. I sprained my ankle.

HALLECK: You're an accountant, Miss Larish. Do you know of any clients who would want you dead?

LARISH: That's a silly question.

HALLECK: Were you ever married?

LARISH: Once. When I was nineteen. Divorced three years later.

HALLECK: Where is your ex-husband now?

LARISH: I don't know. Seattle, I think.

HALLECK: Any children?

LARISH: No.

HALLECK: Are you a woman who makes friends easily?

LARISH: I like to think of myself that way.

HALLECK: Any enemies?

LARISH: I don't think so.

HALLECK: Let me go back to the bus ride for a moment. You said you did notice the woman twice. Both times briefly; once during the ride itself and once when she was standing in the back door with the gun drawn.

LARISH: That's right.

HALLECK: Well, why did you look at her that first time? I mean, what was there about her that drew your eyes?

LARISH: Oh, I don't know.

HALLECK: Was she particularly well dressed?

LARISH: No.

HALLECK: Did she look disturbed in any way?

LARISH: No.

HALLECK: Threatening in any way?

LARISH: No. No.

HALLECK: She was kind of underdressed for the weather. It was cold outside.

LARISH: It was probably just the cat carrier. That's all.

HALLECK: You like cats?

LARISH: Yes.

HALLECK: You have a cat?

LARISH: No.

HALLECK: Okay. I won't bother you anymore now, Miss Larish. Thanks. Hope you feel better fast.

Then Halleck shut down the minirecorder, put the chair back against the wall, and exited. I followed him out.

The moment we were outside, I said: "She didn't realize I was on the bus with her."

"Yeah," he agreed.

"Isn't that strange?"

"Yeah," he agreed.

We walked to the elevator together. He pushed the DOWN button.

Then he turned to me, grinning, and said: "She seems to have seen a different shooter than you."

"I saw what I saw," I replied.

"And she saw what she saw. Only her shooter was a little heavier and had longer hair and Asian eyes."

I didn't respond.

He said: "Maybe we ought to get another sketch drawn up. Maybe there were really two shooters. Maybe they were standing right next to each other. And Alice Nestleton kind of focused on one of the shooters and forgot about the other one. And the lady in the hospital bed focused on the shooter you forgot and in turn forgot the other one. It gets real interesting, doesn't it? How many shooters can pull how many guns out of how many shopping bags on how many buses? You get my drift?"

"Maybe if you knew how to question someone, Detective Halleck, you wouldn't get so many disparities in eyewitness testimony."

Oh, it was a nasty thing to say, but I was very happy I said it.

He burst out laughing. "Is that what Nessem told you?"

"No, this is from me."

"I'm impressed. And how does the famous Cat Woman think I should conduct my interrogations?"

"Well, for one, you didn't ask the woman anything about the shopping bag the shooter was carrying or the clothes the shooter was wearing. That's sloppy."

"Did you say—sloppy?"

"That's what I said."

"You mean sloppy like a guy who forgets to button his fly?"

"If the shoe fits . . ."

"Or do you mean sloppy like a woman who sees a murder and can't provide a simple description of the shooter who was standing right in front of her?"

"Sloppy is sloppy. Any definition you want."

The elevator came. We got on. The door closed. We headed down.

He seemed now to be evaluating my critique seriously. He didn't say a word until we got to the lobby.

"I think, Miss Nestleton, or Cat Woman, or

whatever the hell you call yourself—that you ought to have heard or read somewhere that police officers attempting to establish a perp I.D. based on a police sketch of a face should not confuse an eyewitness by asking questions about the perp's clothing or baggage."

He strode out of the building, leaving me behind. I slowed down, thoroughly chastised.

Detective Halleck turned back once to stare at me through the glass.

Lord, the man despised me. I wondered why.

Then he tapped the side of his head with two fingers. I couldn't figure out what that signified. That I was crazy? That he had my number? What?

Chapter 10

There is no doubt in my mind that from the moment the bus tragedy occurred up to the moment I was in the hospital room monitoring a preliminary interrogation of Natasha Larish by Detective Halleck, I was running on empty, as they say. I was listless. I was flat. Everything about my thought processes and my actions was dull.

Now that is very strange. Look what was happening to me!

Living through a horrendous shooting. Starting a new affair. Dumping an old and profoundly disturbed lover. Completing and waiting for the audience response to what might be a major TV series. Being rehired by RETRO after so many years of what was essentially scorn.

How could one be flat and listless in the face of all that?

Perhaps it was depression. But I think it was

the playing out of shock following the bus shooting.

And so, when, the day after my visit with Halleck to the hospital, I went in to RETRO and discarded all that flatness and flung myself body and soul into my work—I was not slipping over depression to mania.

I am not a manic-depressive.

Let's just say I had stopped pursuing the beef-steak, stopped seasoning it, stopped trimming it—and bit into the bloody thing.

The first thing I did was call Detective Logan and get the name of the M14 bus driver.

The name was Jerry Bock.

Then Logan gave me the name of the Transit Authority unit where bus drivers could be contacted.

I made the call to that MTA unit about ten in the morning. I was routed from line to line until I reached the proper supervisor, who told me that Bock was driving at the time . . . and what was this concerning? I informed him it was police business, that Bock should contact me as quickly as possible, and I left my number. The supervisor told me he would make sure the dispatcher got the message, who would then without a doubt relay the message to Bock.

By the way, he was still driving on the M14 run.

I waited for five hours. I never received any call.

So I went into the CID database and found Bock's phone number at home, which I began to ring. There was no answer. The file said he had a wife, but she was definitely not home.

The file also said that Mr. Bock moonlighted several afternoons a week at a place called the Sun Hospice for the Terminally Ill. Located on West 91st Street, between West End and Riverside, it was affiliated with the United Church of Christ.

At four o'clock, still not having heard from Bock, I left RETRO and headed toward the Sun Hospice.

Like I said, in a few short hours I had been transmogrified into a demon . . . from a flathead.

Now, as I was subwaying uptown, I suddenly remembered a series of dreams I had experienced the previous evening. It was funny that I had not remembered them until I got on a moving vehicle—because the dreams were all about buses.

In the dreams, which were very short but many, people are getting on and off buses carrying shopping bags and cat carriers. All kinds of people. My grandmother. My niece and her husband. My friends. Tony with a crazy hat. All of them getting on and getting off—but always through the rear doors.

In these mini-dreams I am watching the peo-

ple board and disembark and I have some kind
of little counter in my hand. I am pressing a
button on the counter to record whether or not
I think each boarding person has a gun in his
or her shopping bag and whether each person
leaving has discharged a gun.

My counting activity in the mini-dreams is
very quiet and academic and orderly, except at
the very end of each dream, when I am tallying
the numbers for that specific bus. At the end I
am filled with dread, and then I wake up. And
when I get back to sleep it starts all over again.
On and on it goes for what seems like hours.

I had no idea how to interpret these dreams,
but once I remembered them, there on the subway, I was absolutely sure that the sudden
change in my behavior, the almost wild vigor,
the persistence, was due in some way to those
dreams and my remembering most of them.

There were no marks or signs on the tall, well-
kept brownstone that identified it as the final
stop for the terminally ill.

But there was a brightly burnished brass
knocker on the outside door. An incongruous
item in Manhattan these days, but made less so
by the macabre aspect of it—the hooded man
with the scythe always knocks, doesn't he?

I hit the knocker three times against the wood
door and then chuckled to myself when I heard

the low tick of a surveillance apparatus. In a few seconds the latch disengaged; I pushed the heavy door open and stepped inside.

The rooms had the spare look of a typical doctor's office: minimal furnishings, magazines scattered about, a few file cabinets, and a faintly antiseptic smell in the air. I closed the door behind me and wandered a few feet into the hallway.

The place was very unnaturally quiet. There was a staircase and an elevator—one of those small ones occasionally found in brownstones remodeled for offices or to suit the needs of elderly residents.

I heard a door open and close and then a tall, heavyset woman, perhaps ten years older than I, approached me.

She was wearing a kind of modified nurse's garb, but she was capless, her light-colored hair pulled back in a small bun.

There was a name tag pinned to her outfit which I was able to read when she came close: LILA GIBBONS.

She had several pamphlets or booklets in one hand.

"May I help you?" she asked, polite but cool.

"This is the Sun Hospice. Isn't it?" I inquired.

"Yes. But we really don't encourage people walking in off the street," she replied.

Then she handed me two pamphlets and

added kindly, "Why don't you call for an appointment?"

"No. No. I'm not here making inquiries about hospice care."

Her mood changed quickly. Now I was merely an intruder—maybe a door-to-door saleswoman.

"Then how may I help you?"

"Does a man named Jerry Bock work here?"

"Why do you ask?"

"I have to contact him."

"About what? Is he in some kind of difficulty?"

She seemed to be getting more and more agitated. I didn't want to alienate her. To me, anyone who works in a hospice is an excellent human being because hospices, which alleviate the suffering of the dying and their loved ones, are probably the most wonderful institutions ever conceived and developed by humankind. Quite simply, I loved them and supported them.

So I figured it was time to identify myself.

I handed her my brand-new RETRO photo I.D. card, assuring her that Mr. Bock was in no difficulty whatsoever.

She studied the card carefully, matched the face on the card and the face in front of her, then handed it back.

"Jerry Bock is one of our drivers. He transports patients to the hospice and similar work."

"Is he working today?"

"Yes. He's out on a run."

"Can I wait for him?"

She nodded and beckoned me to follow her down the hall, which I did. She ushered me into a small, well-furnished room

"You can stay here, Officer," she said.

I didn't correct her. I sat down on a high-backed, beautifully upholstered chair now going to tatters.

Lila Gibbons started to leave, reconsidered, and turned back toward me. "The hospice," she said, "is situated in the building next door. This is just an annex. I'll leave a note there for Mr. Bock that you are waiting for him."

"Thank you."

"You know, he is a very nice man," she noted.

"I'm sure he is."

"I can't believe he's done anything criminal."

"He hasn't," I assured her. "There are just some questions I need answered. About something he saw several years ago while driving a bus. Believe me, it does not pertain to his work at the hospice."

That seemed to satisfy her, but she still said as she was leaving: "And he shouldn't be harassed."

I settled in and read several pieces of literature about the hospice movement in general and the Sun Hospice in particular.

Forty minutes later the door opened and Jerry Bock entered. A bony man in his mid-forties with a shaved head and a moustache, he seemed bewildered by my presence.

"What is this about?" he asked.

"Detective Logan gave me your name."

"Who?"

"The detective in charge of that situation . . . a few years ago . . . on your bus."

That clued him in. "Add dead and buried," he said gruffly.

"No. Alive and well," I contradicted, "because of its resemblance to the recent murders on the M8 line."

"You must be kidding. No one was killed on my bus. Nothing happened, lady."

"Look. Do me a favor. Just tell me what happened."

"Didn't that detective tell you?"

"Yes. But Logan wasn't driving the bus. I want to hear it from you."

"Fine. Let's get it over with. I'll tell you what I remember. It was, I think, a Wednesday morning. Winter. The bus, going east, wasn't that crowded. I stop for a light at Irving Place. . . ."

"Wait!" I interrupted. A lightbulb went off in my head. I knew the 14th Street line. Irving was basically only a block and a half east of Broadway over there. Another possible coincidence.

"Are you sure of the bus location at the time?" I asked.

"Yeah. That's about the only thing I am sure about, because I remember staring at the sale signs on the P.C. Richards store windows. Anyway, I'm waiting there for the light to turn green. And then this lady seems to pop out of nowhere, right beside me, real close. Strange-looking lady . . . like a beat-up hawk she looks . . . maybe sixty. She tells me a passenger was about to get off the bus at Broadway with a shopping bag. But at the last minute she don't get off. She pulls a gun out of the shopping bag, points it at seated passengers, and pulls the trigger. Only nothing happens. She runs off the bus. That's it."

"What did you do?"

"Well, I looked back in the bus. No one seemed disturbed at all. No one seemed shaken up. The passengers weren't stirred up and talking to each other. Nothing. So I figured the lady telling me the story was some kind of a nut, just another New York crazy. Then she gives me a couple of cans of cat food that she said the passenger with the gun left on the bus. No, wait. She said the cans fell out of the shopping bag when the gun was pulled out of the bag."

He paused as if trying to remember something crucial.

"Anything else?"

"No. I was just remembering. Anyway, that was that. When I finished my run I reported the incident. The cops found that hawk lady and questioned her. I don't think they ever found anyone else on the bus to confirm or deny the hawk lady's story. They did get a vague description of the lady with the gun from the hawk lady, but it wasn't much. I didn't remember anyone like that on the bus."

"What kind of cat food was it?"

"Funny-looking cans, heart shaped. I remember reading the label on one of them—sardine and shrimp. I remember thinking to myself how times have changed, how house cats live real good now."

"What happened to them?"

"The cans? I don't know."

"Can't you tell me anything else, Mr. Bock?"

"No. Not really."

"The woman who walked up to you and reported what supposedly happened—she died recently."

"I'm sorry, but I really didn't know her and after that one time, I never saw her again."

"You didn't think she was deranged when she first spoke to you, did you? Wasn't it only when you saw that there was no disorder at all in the bus?"

"I suppose so. But she did act strange from the start."

"Like a hawk?" I teased him.

"Yeah."

And that was the end of my interview with Jerry Bock. It was not a total blank. There was now the similarity—the Broadway connection. Was it valid? Meaningful? I didn't know. But it did add a piece—in both incidents the gunwoman had exited at or near Broadway.

Would it please Nessem?

The problem was, what to do next?

I thanked the bus driver. He left. I called Les Rawls. He was at home. He suggested I come over since I was already on the Upper West Side.

He said that he would make supper for me, that he would impress me to hell with his ability to construct an omelet.

He said that I had to spend the night or he would be very sad. Since I never liked causing sadness in other people, particularly fellow actors, I agreed.

Remember the line in that old song . . . something about the night being a lovely tune . . . and that one should be careful of such thoughts if one has a foolish heart.

Guilty as charged! It was a melodious night with Les.

And, as dawn broke, we both had foolish hearts by any stretch of the clichéd imagination.

Of course, we're both in the theater and that's expected. Whatever one's age, fantasy brings forth fantasy.

We had a cup of coffee together, sitting side by side like two satiated children watching tugboats on the Hudson River through the window.

Then he went back to sleep.

I stood at the window, wearing one of his shirts. I thought for a moment of Tony, but only for a moment.

I watched the current move.

The melody and the calmness seemed to be slipping away.

Why? I didn't know. Everything was going well for me. A new lover. A new television series. A new job. What more did I want? How greedy had I become? Had the Cat Woman gone Hollywood? Had I become grasping? Insatiable? Had I lost a sense of my limits?

My mind was becoming like Swiss cheese. Thoughts were moving in and out without getting resolved.

The wind was starting to pick up outside, banging against the windows. I stepped back a bit but could still see the river.

Should I get another coffee? Should I go back to bed? Should I get dressed now and go home and feed Bushy and Pancho and talk to them a bit and try to find out what they were thinking about my life?

I burst out laughing. The cats always brought me back to reality.

And my reality right now was an investigation that was going nowhere fast.

Nessem was really not going to be impressed at the fact that I might have uncovered another link between the M8 and M14 incidents . . . that both had happened at Broadway six blocks and three years from each other . . . a very fragile connection.

I spotted a piece of debris moving downtown; it looked like the smashed hull of a rowboat. Watching it bounce and turn in the swift current, I remembered a story Sam Tully had told me, about when he was a kid living on the Lower East Side. He used to spend hours by the Hudson. Winter was his favorite time because there were always ice floes on the water drifting toward the bay and sometimes he would see birds riding the floes—mostly eagles and hawks.

They were just hitchhikers, enjoying a free ride. Then came DDT.

The raptors on the floes disappeared. The moment I recalled that story, I remembered another hawk reference.

A woman as hawk.

At least that was how the bus driver described his informant on the M14 that day.

Oh, there was no doubt about it. I had to look into the life and death of the hawk lady.

*   *   *

At the RETRO staff meeting the next morning, my new connection was disclosed and discussed. Then Nessem suggested that the witness revenge angle pertaining to the dead school-teacher didn't seem to be going anywhere.

And then he gave us a little pep talk.

"Keep pushing!" he said.

"We're getting closer!" he said.

"We'll have an I.D. soon on the shooter," he predicted.

I went back to my desk and called Detective Logan and asked him for the name and last known address of the deceased hawk lady.

Logan was nice. He faxed me the very slim file, which contained full name, date of birth, address work history (almost nonexistent), and a verbatim transcript of her statement about what happened on the M14 bus that day, including her pathetic attempts to provide a description of the "shooter," a hodgepodge of contradictory comments . . . "maybe tall . . . maybe not . . . maybe dressed in a pantsuit . . . maybe wearing a tweed suit . . . maybe Italian . . . maybe Hispanic . . . maybe thirty . . . maybe fifty."

The deceased woman's name was Teresa Positi.

And she had lived all her life on Rivington Street, in the heart of the old Lower East Side of Manhattan.

There was one photo of Teresa Positi in the file; it showed a woman who looked more like a bedraggled sparrow than a hawk. In the photo, taken in front of some kind of clothing store, Teresa had a shawl on her head, a bunch of flowers in her hand, and she was wearing a long yellow summer dress.

A note attached to the photo, obviously in Logan's hand, stated that it was taken only a year or so before her death. The cause of death was a heart attack. Her age was 71.

I left the office at eleven-thirty in the morning, after having received my Tulip report back from Nessem with his comments, written in small red margin notes—"Interesting. Please expand."

Obviously he was a bit disappointed in the Cat Woman's interrogation of Tulip and her interpretation of the interrogation.

I walked from Beaver Street to Rivington in about an hour, stopping off for a quick, large, inexpensive, and delicious bowl of Shanghai noodle soup on East Broadway.

The first thing I noticed on the corner was the clothing shop that was in the file photo, the one Teresa Positi had posed in front of.

The sign, which was not visible in the photo, read: EVERGREEN CLOTHES—NEW AND USED.

It was not open and there was no notice on the door or window to inform the passerby as to the reason it was closed.

I walked around the corner to the small gray three-story building where Teresa Positi had spent her life.

The first floor housed a wholesale flooring distributor. There were two young men working inside. I showed them the photo. They gave me blank looks. They didn't know the woman who had lived overhead until last year.

I walked to the curb and stared up. The file had noted that Teresa lived on the second floor. There were only four windows facing the street on each floor and since the bottom floor, the first floor, was a shuttered wholesaler, there were only windows on the second and third floor—eight in all.

As I stood there I noticed that someone on the third floor was staring down at me. Because of the glare from the bright winter sun I could not see very well . . . but it was a person and there was something in the person's arms.

I shifted my spot on the street to get out of the glare and could see more clearly. It was a woman and she was standing in the window and there was a cat on her shoulder.

I waved. The woman didn't respond. I waved again, more emphatically. The woman opened the window—I could see she was old—and stuck her head out. The cat leaped off her shoulder and vanished.

She yelled: "Who are you?"

"A friend of Teresa's," I yelled back.

"I don't know you!" she yelled.

"Can I come up?"

At first my request seemed to frighten her. Then she vanished from the window for a moment, only to reappear with the cat in her arms. She stroked the beast nervously as she stared down silently. "Okay. Okay."

I walked to the cramped lobby and saw by the mailboxes that there were indeed two apartments on each floor. Teresa's name had been scratched off one of them. I had no idea which of the other three names was the window lady.

Then the buzzer sounded. I walked through and began to climb. When I reached the second floor I heard a voice call out: "One more. One more."

She was there to meet me on the third-floor landing. An old woman, rawboned, face like a railroad track, wisps of white hair flying every which way. The cat in her arms was making a terrible racket. He was a big yellow-and-white thug with tiny ears.

"Now tell me who you really are," she said, a bit threateningly.

I decided to tell the truth. I flashed my laminated RETRO I.D. and she squinted at it.

"What does it mean?"

"Teresa witnessed an incident on a bus three

years ago. She told the police what happened. People laughed at her. People thought she was crazy. I believe her. And I'm trying to find out more."

The woman laughed. "More what? She's dead."

"I know she's dead," I replied.

The woman and the cat stared at me. She said: "My name is Fran. I've lived here for twenty years. I went shopping with Teresa three days a week. We went to the Essex Street market sometimes. And sometimes we went to the pork store on Mulberry Street. You know it?"

"No." I admitted.

She took me by the arm and guided me into the apartment, her cat glaring at me from the safety of her shoulder.

It was a lovely little apartment and stuffed with all kinds of irrelevancies, like small refrigerators that obviously weren't being used, and a very intricate folding bed on which were stacked magazines.

I sat down in a comfortable easy chair that was covered with a bright blue-and-white flower pattern. The cat jumped down off Fran and up onto the arm of my chair.

"My name is really not Fran. It's Francine. That's what most people call me. Francine."

"And most people call me Alice."

"My cat is Bobbo."

"That's a nice name," I replied, staring at the brute who was now inspecting me.

"Let's face it. Bobbo isn't pretty. But he gets things done."

"I'm sure he does," I agreed.

"Would you like coffee?"

"No, Francine. I can't stay long. I just want to talk to you about Teresa."

"Talk."

"Was she upset that many people seemed not to believe her story about the bus?"

"I think she was."

"Did she talk to you about it?"

"Of course. All the time. See, she thought God had intervened to save her life and those of the other people on the bus. She thought that woman was gong to kill them all."

"Tell me, Francine, you knew her well . . . was Teresa a woman with a vivid imagination?"

"You mean was she a liar?"

"No. Not at all. I mean did she have a tendency to embellish?"

"Oh, you're barking up the wrong tree. Not Teresa." And here Francine crossed herself before continuing. "She lost her husband years ago. She lost a child. She was a very down-to-earth person. She knew what was going on."

That last comment confused me. What did Francine mean?

She came toward me quickly then and for some reason plucked the cat off the chair and sent him scurrying away, wailing.

She wagged her finger at me. "You do not understand what a wonderful woman she was. But even she had her limits."

"What limits do you mean?"

"Oh, come on! You know they abused her after that."

"Who abused her?"

"The police."

"You mean after the trouble on the bus?"

"Of course that's what I mean. They made her get a psychiatric examination."

"I'm sorry that happened."

"And that's why she walked away."

"From helping the police?"

"Yes."

Suddenly Francine became gloomy and agitated and started gesturing to herself, as if she were having a secret hostile conversation.

"But she did do something wrong and she knew it," Francine said. "Oh, she knew it as sure as the day is long and she was sorry about it."

I knew that I was on the cusp of something important. I had to be careful. I had to keep her talking. I had to keep her confidence. It was obvious she was taking me somewhere.

She started to inspect me very carefully, peering up and down my body as if evaluating me for some task.

Then she got herself an apple and knife and sat down on a chair near me and placed a large napkin on her lap and began to peel the apple.

"Would you like some?" she asked.

"No. I just ate."

She peeled the apple in one unbroken strand and then cored it and ate the fruit with relish, all the while squinting her eyes to evaluate me further.

When she was finished she said a prolonged "aah" and then crumpled the napkin with all the residue into a ball.

"There is something you should understand about Teresa," she said conspiratorially. "When she was little, she was a lot of trouble. We went to school together. On Elizabeth Street. Oh, the nuns had a lot of problems with her. She would steal. Not big things, mind you. Little things. Pens, handkerchiefs, pieces of candy."

She paused there, waiting for some kind of response. I didn't know what to say.

She continued: "But that was when she was a little girl. She stopped doing that. She became a saint. Many people in the neighborhood thought Teresa was a saint. Did you know that?"

"No."

Now Francine seemed to be suffering some kind of inner conflict. She started to speak again, then stopped. She looked at the ceiling and the floor . . . she started to squeeze the balled-up napkin . . . she did all kinds of strange things.

Finally she got up and beckoned me with a finger to follow her. We walked into her bedroom. She motioned that I should stand by the bed and wait. She went into the closet and pulled out a large carton.

She heaved it onto the bed, amazingly spry for a woman her age, and dumped out the contents.

"All that is left of Teresa," she muttered.

There were some clothes, a few hats, a few pieces of jewelry in a clear plastic bag, and several pairs of shoes. At least that was all I could see at first.

Francine dug into the pile and pulled out a book.

"Take it," she said.

I took the book.

"Look at it," she said.

I studied the book. It was one of those large-format children's books, titled *Frogs and Toads of the World*. The cover was shiny and waterproof and a huge bullfrog on a lily pad stared at the reader. Inside were portraits, crudely but colorfully drawn, of various frogs and toads found throughout the world, and under each toad or frog was a brief description of the life cycle, habitat, and peculiarities of the creature.

It was the kind of book one always sees on the tables of those street peddlers in Manhattan.

"It was just something that happened," Francine said.

"To whom?"

"To Teresa. She was frightened. She became a child again. She stole."

"From whom?"

"The woman on the bus."

"You mean the woman on *that* bus . . . the one who Teresa said took out a gun . . . the one who dropped the cat food cans. She also dropped this?"

"Dropped—left—I don't know which. But it was hers and Teresa took it. And she never told the police. But she did tell me."

I sat down suddenly on the bed. Did you ever get weak from wonderment?

Chapter 11

I placed the frog-and-toad book that Francine had given me in the center of the table.

Sam Tully stared at it and shrugged. "What am I supposed to do with this, Nestleton?"

"Just take a look," I said.

He took a sip of beer, wiped his hands with a napkin, and began to study it. As he did so, I told him the circumstances of its acquisition.

We had just consumed hamburgers at the Corner Bistro on Jane Street. It was a place Sam went when he desired a very good hamburger. I had devoured mine with a kind of nervous intensity. Sometimes one feels, as I do, that only a good hamburger can restore balance to one's existence.

He finished studying the book, pushed it back toward me, and said, "Can I deal with something else first?"

"Go ahead."

"Now, I don't want you to take this wrong,

honey, but I'd really like to know why you don't look like you're in love."

"Should I, Sam?"

"Well, you are sleeping with this guy Harry, aren't you?"

"His name is Lester, Sam. Lester Rawls. People call him Les."

"Fine. Les. I like the name. It's easy to remember, easy to forget. So, honey, what's the story?"

Sam lit a cigarette, sat back in the booth, exhaled hugely, and gave me one of his sly, obnoxious looks.

"Yes, I am sleeping with him. Yes, I think maybe I have started to love him. But if what you say is true and I don't look like I'm in love, I don't know how to explain it. Maybe because I have a lot more on the table."

"Tony been bothering you?"

"No. I haven't seen him or heard from him."

"Poor bastard," Sam muttered.

I didn't respond. I sipped my stein of Bass Ale. Was I in love with Les? At my age, I know that love is an idiotic term to describe what goes on between this woman and a specific man. The only category was need. Did I need him? Did he need me? And did my face reflect that need? When Sam said there was no love in my eyes, did he mean no need? Did I need Lester Rawls now the way I had once needed Tony? To live, to prosper, to feel good, to feel happy, to feel pleasure, to feel worth, to feel work. Uh-oh. I was getting deeper into this nonsense.

I picked up the frog-and-toad book and shook it.

"Do you think it's significant?" I asked.

"Significant? You're starting to sound like a Method actress again."

"That's what I am. An old Method actress. Love me or leave me, Sam."

He found that very funny and picked up the book again and began to leaf through it.

"Look, honey. A picture of an Oak Toad. It says the Oak Toad is the smallest toad in North America."

He looked at several other toads and frogs and commented on their salient points. He was beginning to mock me again, in a genial fashion.

"Here's my problem, Sam. Why didn't Teresa Positi show this book to the cops? Supposedly that woman who drew a gun on the M14 left behind several cans of cat food and this book. Teresa gave the cops the cans and kept the book. Why? Was it because she had a history of petty thievery as a child and the sight of this book suddenly triggered that old behavior pattern? Probably. Don't you agree?"

"It's possible. Maybe probable."

"And why was the lady carrying it in the first place, along with the cat food cans? Was it a present for a grandchild?"

"Who knows, Nestleton? But people who plan shootings usually travel light."

"And maybe, Sam, this Teresa Positi, when she was alive, never told the truth to anyone. Maybe she obtained the cans and the book before she boarded the M14 bus that day. And maybe she was the woman shooter, in her fantasy, and she projected herself in the bus stairwell, firing away."

"Maybe, maybe, maybe, honey. It's a stupid word."

I finished my stein of ale.

"Have another one," Sam suggested.

"No, thanks."

He ordered another for himself. The bistro was becoming crowded with young people. Sam and I stood out like something time forgot.

I picked the frog-and-toad children's book up off the table and returned it to my bag.

"How long is your contract at RETRO?" Sam asked.

"Well, I was hired on a six-week contract, but, if I remember, RETRO always automatically renews at least once. So I'm there for a minimum of twelve weeks."

"Why don't you just get out of there after your first contract is up. Or before. You don't need the money anymore."

"Just quit?"

"Yeah."

"Why?"

"To be honest, it looks to me like you're going nowhere but into the natural history of toads."

"But that's because Nessem assigned me to the M14 incident. I should be investigating a multiple murder on the M8. One that I witnessed."

"Agreed. But this Nessem won't change his mind, Nestleton. I never met the guy, but from what you told me he's easy to read. Wanted to show people that RETRO was open enough to rehire the notorious Cat Woman, though her techniques were on the feline occult level. And wants to use said Cat Woman to come up with a cockamamie theory tying the two buses together because one lady with a gun left a cat in a carrier and the other left some cat food cans. The quote tying together unquote would validate RETRO involvement in what should be just a case for a homicide squad. You see what I'm saying?"

He was getting me in a very depressed mood. I knew what he was saying was true . . . I had thought it before he articulated it . . . but I had avoided the conclusion.

"Another reason to quit, honey, is because the whole thing is going nowhere. Am I right?"

"That I can't predict. The one good lead we had—about one of the victims being a witness in an old felony case—didn't work out. If it had, we would have known that the old school-teacher was the intended victim, and the motive was vengeance."

"Look. Get real. If you people don't I.D. the shooter on the M8, you're going nowhere. And I don't think you're going to do it. Like you said, even the sketch lacks authenticity. It's a dead end. Tulip is a dead end. You can't dig up the motive. And if there was no rational motive, you can't dig up a psychotic shooter without a real face or real prints or a traceable object. I figure the case will shut down as soon as the hubbub dies. And maybe three years from now the weapon will turn up by chance and poof—the gun will be tied to a dealer or another shooter and then traced to some loony in a nut ward upstate and that will be that. Time and luck. Like most crimes like this. Definitely not mystery novel stuff. And most definitely not Cat Woman stuff."

"Why do I get the feeling, Sam, that you have some kind of handle on this mess but you're keeping quiet?"

"A handle?"

"Yes. That you have some kind of insight that you think would correct the wrong path RETRO is taking."

He smiled at me but did not reply. Smile? Maybe it was closer to a smirk.

I suddenly noticed a young couple across the

aisle from us and two booths down. They were staring at Sam and me with great interest and making comments to each other.

I wondered what had piqued their interest in us.

Were Sam and I one of those Manhattan scenes so beloved of *New Yorker* readers? An old derelict raising his voice while explaining something to a cool and leggy blonde many years his junior?

Both players a bit tipsy. Both a bit eccentric.

The watching couple suddenly noticed me watching them watch me—and turned their gaze away quickly.

Sam said, finally, "Okay. To tell the truth, I think I got something."

"Spit it out, Sam. We're all friends here. You didn't have any trouble telling me how futile the investigation is."

"You were on that bus, weren't you, honey? Right there . . . in the center of the maelstrom?"

"Yes."

"And a lot of other people were with you?"

"Yes."

"And all you people saw a lot. Particularly you."

"We saw almost everything, but we saw through a glass darkly. We couldn't even agree on the face of the killer."

"And now you're working with RETRO and

you have access to the most sophisticated computer in the world of criminal investigation."

"So they say."

"And with all this, all these observations and machines and human resources, you're getting nowhere fast."

"We all agree on that."

"It's time, Nestleton, to get a little avant-garde. Maybe something like Ionesco's *Rhinoceros*. You remember that play, Nestleton? Or was that before your time? A little twisty we have to get. A little speculative. A little nuanced."

"Nuanced?"

"I love that word, honey. Don't you? Now, listen. I am going to make a pronouncement."

I waited. But first he nuanced himself with another cigarette and another beer. It was nice to see the old goat happy. Sam was a very smart man. When he was happy as well as smart, it was a rather potent combination.

"I'm listening, Sam," I prodded.

"I think the best thing to do . . . the best way to go about this . . . is to engage in a little Socratic dialogue, honey."

"Anything you say, Sam."

"Let's go back to the event."

"What event?"

"The one you saw . . . the one you experienced . . . the one you were immersed in.

The shooting on your M8 bus. So think now, honey."

"I told you everything, Sam."

"Yeah, yeah. So you say. But you never told me what about the event stank of illogic."

"Everything. Nothing about it was logical. Nothing was normal. Sam, it was horrendous—an atrocity. Aren't you aware of that?"

"I'm aware that it was an atrocity. But the moment the bullets were fired . . . the moment after . . . you were all back in the real rational world of people responding to an event. Get my drift?"

"No."

"What was illogical in the behavior of the people on the bus after the shooting . . . right after . . . after the shooter exited the bus?"

"Nothing. Everyone just responded to the event. What I did wasn't logical or illogical. I acted automatically. I was in shock."

"Did you help the wounded and dying?"

"No. Not really."

"Why not?"

"Like I said. I was in shock."

"So in a sense you acted logically. Many people, in the presence of sudden violence, go into a kind of protective shock. It's logical."

"Okay, Sam. Where is this Socratic dialogue going?"

"You're not thinking deep, honey. There *was* one very large breach in the logic of the situation."

"Which was?"

"Chasing the shooter."

"What was illogical about that? One of the people on the bus is so enraged at what he saw that he wants to get the person who did the damage. He runs after her. Two people follow him. The killer shoots the young man dead. The young man was a hero."

"You think so?"

"Yes. Of course. His name was Calvin Rupp. He was a thirty-one-year-old law student, and he gave up his life trying to apprehend a killer. If that wasn't heroic, I don't know what is."

"You never read my last book, did you, honey? Where Harry Bondo gets shot in the leg chasing some perp. A cop says Harry is one brave man. And Harry Bondo laughs so hard he pisses his pants."

"No, I never read that one, Sam."

"The kid, this Rupp, should have first attended to the people who were shot. A hero would've done that."

"Oh, come on, Sam. That's a stretch."

"The logic of the situation requires all persons witnessing a horrendous shooting to give aid and comfort to the victim. This is primary. So, I ask what motivated this Rupp to take off after the shooter, without a weapon to match hers. Maybe the kid was just a wild man? But no, law students are not wild men."

"At thirty-one he really wasn't a kid. Maybe he just reacted instinctively as a hero because that was his nature. Just a rage against injustice."

"Maybe. But maybe he would have saved one or two of the dead, as well as himself, if he had stayed around."

"This is second-guessing."

"Sure it is. But what the hell is criminal investigation if you don't throw out options."

"To be honest, Sam, I don't follow this option you're developing. Are you saying RETRO should look at Rupp as some kind of conspirator in the shooting?"

"Is that crazy?"

"Yes. The RETRO computer did a detailed profile of everyone shot on that bus to look for a shooter motive. I'm talking about an in-depth profile. There was nothing there."

"Computers are stupid, honey. They're looking for the wrong thing. And they find it. Besides, all I'm saying is, my gut says—take a look at this hero named Rupp."

"Look, Sam, even if you're right, it doesn't help me. Nessem told me he wants me to work on the M14 incident, to prove a connection between the two."

"Like I said, honey, maybe you ought to quit now. Or, of course, you can keep interviewing cats in shelters and collecting books on frogs and toads."

The tone of his voice, the sarcastic grin, infuriated me. I had a sudden desire to hit him over the head with one of the empty steins on the table. And then I felt ashamed of myself. I mean, he was sunk in his booth, his grizzled white beard like a halo, his jacket with the broken zipper draped over his shoulders. In a sense, he had taken the place of my grandmother, who raised me on that grim dairy farm in Minnesota. Yes, good old Grandma Sam Tully. Surely I couldn't hit him in the head with a Bass Ale stein.

Besides, he had a point.

"Okay, Sam, I'll take a surreptitious look at the hero."

"Good."

"And maybe you'll take a peek with me, Sam."

"What else do I have to do, Nestleton?"

Chapter 12

I obtained a seven-page profile of the dead young man, Calvin Rupp, from the Criminal Investigation Database. You can imagine how long it would have been if there had been anything criminal in Rupp's background.

There wasn't. Not a traffic ticket, not a summons for spitting on the sidewalk; he'd never even been kept after school.

He was born and raised in Brooklyn, New York, attended Grady Vocational High School, then Long Island University at night, and, at the time of his death, was a student at CUNY Law, in his third year.

His parents were from St. Lucia and had arrived in this country in the 1950s as children; they married in 1967 and produced Calvin in 1970. Both parents were now deceased.

The database noted and recorded and provided replicas of the various pieces of paper that had defined him:

Student I.D. cards at LIU and the law school
Public and school library cards
Social Security card
Driver's license
Medical insurance card
Credit cards

The really astonishing aspect of the CID was that all this information had been obtained without a registered set of fingerprints for Calvin Rupp because he had never been arrested or been in the Army, Navy, or Marines.

The profile also provided a work history.

According to the printout, Calvin Rupp's work record was consistent with a longtime struggling student: delivery boy at D'Agostino; phone marketer; bike messenger; school cafeteria server; bookstore clerk; and summer lifeguard at a municipal pool.

I met Sam for lunch at the South Street Seaport. We sat on the top glass-enclosed deck of one of the fast-food piers. Sam ate a chili dog as he perused the document. I had a cup of tea and an order of the worst french fries I had ever tasted.

Sam read the document carefully between bites.

When he was finished, he handed it back to me delicately.

"Impressive?" I asked.

"In some ways," he admitted.

"In some ways? Come on, Sam! It's an astonishing amount of information pulled out of thin air."

"There's a problem, Nestleton."

"Which is?"

"After reading this, do you know the hero any better?"

"Sure you do. For one, we know where he worked."

"No, you don't. For every job listed here, he probably worked at three others off the books and they are not found there."

"Okay. That's probably true. But it also gives you his complete school record."

"Get real, honey. Look at the guy's photo. Light-skinned black man about six-one, conservative dresser, small eyes, no moustache, big brow, fastidious short haircut. I look at him and I say to myself, Well, well, young Rupp. Who do you hang with? Who do you sleep with? What do you eat? What do you think? Where do you drink?"

I was suddenly embarrassed at my enthusiasm for the RETRO sheets. Sam was absolutely right.

"So what do we do if we continue this?"

"I don't like your attitude, honey. You think this Rupp was a garden-variety hero. You think there is no way he could be anything else. You think my intuition is like a bad joke—forget the whole bloody thing. You're not doing me a favor, honey, remember that."

"Calm down, Sam. Yes, I want to pursue this. But how?"

"Well, like Harry Bondo says, there are only two things important in a good man's life: who he's sleeping with and who he's drinking with."

"Like you said, Sam. RETRO doesn't provide that."

"We can get there."

"How?"

"Because there's something very strange about our martyred hero."

"What?"

Sam grabbed the first sheet back and pointed to the last known address of Calvin Rupp.

It read: 18 Voorhees Court, Brooklyn.

"What's strange about the address, Sam?"

"Your hero lived in Sheepshead Bay."

"So?"

"It's a long way from where he went to school. It's a long train ride anywhere."

"Maybe he liked the neighborhood."

"I'm sure he did. It's a nice place, right by the water. The trouble is, it has a reputation of being very inhospitable to people of color."

"Times change, Sam."

"Sure they do. Sure, honey. But there's a better reason for a black man to move to a neighborhood like Sheepshead Bay than trying to integrate it. Maybe he likes to fish."

"I don't understand where you're going with this."

"If you like the water and you like to fish and you're going to law school and you need money, Sheepshead Bay is a good place to live. Because the party boats go out of Sheepshead Bay, and the skippers always need young men to work the boats and they pay good cash for a day's work and they pay it off the books."

I was so taken aback by Sam's rather brilliant flight of possibility that I didn't say anything for a long while. I just stared out at the East River.

But there were some problems. Calvin Rupp had lived in Sheepshead Bay because he liked to fish and work on party boats. So what? How was that going to help us?

Sam picked up on what I was thinking. He said, "If I'm right, honey, it gives us a pool of people who knew this guy. Boat captains, mates, bartenders."

"Bartenders?"

"Sure. All-night bars where the boats pull out and pull in. Remember, these are party boats, not commercial fishermen. Each boat carries anywhere between ten and fifty people who pay to get taken to where the fish are. Before and after, they like to drink? Especially if it's winter, which it is now, and the cod boats go out now and that fishing is night work."

"You think we should go out there, Sam?"

"Yes. I think we should go out there today . . . tonight . . . and wrap it up one way or another. But then again, honey, there's no need to go at all if you don't think there was something funny about our hero."

"I don't know what I think," I said plaintively, realizing to my chagrin that I was sounding like the stereotypical damsel in distress. But, in effect, I was one. "Let's go to Sheepshead Bay," I said.

So that's how I ended up on Emmons Avenue in Sheepshead Bay at ten in the evening on a freezing night.

On one side of the avenue were stores, houses, restaurants, bars.

On the other side were the piers and the party boats moored at them, and shills in front of the piers calling out to motorists and passersby that their boats would bring home the most fish for them.

We headed toward the closest boat, a big ugly thing called the *Captain Tony*.

Sam said, "I better handle this."

I replied, "Right, Sam. I'll just tag along and keep my mouth shut."

Suddenly I was aware of the ridiculousness of my situation. I was prey to two delusional, rather nice idiots. One, Nessem, thought I could extract information from a cat. And the other, Tully, had a bee in his bonnet about the only person in the whole mess who had come out of it smelling sweet—a bona fide hero—Calvin Rupp. May he rest in peace.

We developed a shipboard routine quickly for the six boats that were taking on customers that night. Sam showed the picture of Calvin Rupp obtained from the RETRO database. I showed my RETRO I.D. validating the inquiry. And Sam asked the questions.

The first one was a bust. And the second and third.

The fourth captain—his name was Romeo if I recall correctly—knew Rupp. Rupp had worked these cod runs on his boat four nights a week since Christmas.

Romeo had heard of Rupp's death.

The conversation proceeded thusly:

SAM: You know the kid did a brave thing . . . a very brave thing.

ROMEO: So I hear.

SAM: Did you figure he would do something like that in that kind of situation?

ROMEO: It was hard to tell what Rupp would do. The guy was quiet. Very quiet. But he did his work. The guys on board liked him.

SAM: Did he ever mention a girlfriend?

ROMEO: No. Look, I really didn't know anything about him. He shows up one night asking me for work. He tells me he worked party boats before, which was a lie, but it didn't really matter, because he picked up fast. I don't know anything about him. Once in a while I would see him in Flynn's after we docked.

SAM: What's Flynn's?

ROMEO: A bar on Emmons. Just across the street, about two blocks toward the parkway. He would be sitting in a booth drinking a Coke and eating a sandwich he bought at the all-night luncheonette near the subway.

Right after that conversation, Sam and I went to Flynn's.

The minute I walked in I realized this was a whole new world. The bar was long and high and it had old-fashioned wooden stools. The walls were covered with pictures of old prize-fighters but it was too dark to see their faces. There was no music. There were two ancient televisions hoisted up on either end of the bar, but there was no sound to accompany the picture. There was sawdust on the floor and a stink of seaweed and bad water and salt and fish innards.

The bartender looked like a man newly arrived in Brooklyn—transported there from some penal colony. Of course, he and Sam hit it off immediately.

BARTENDER: He used to come in maybe three times a week. He worked the night party boats. Got here around four. Stayed for a couple of hours. He used to sit in that booth and read, drinking soda and eating sandwiches. He never bought anything alcoholic.

SAM: You see what he was reading?

BARTENDER: Studying. He was always studying law books.

SAM: You ever talk to him?

BARTENDER: Couple of times.

SAM: About what?

BARTENDER: Well, believe it or not, he was a kind of philosopher. We used to talk a lot about dying and things like that.

SAM: It would really help us if you could remember those conversations better.

BARTENDER: Hard to remember. You know. Philosophy. About dying. He had lost both his parents. He talked about his mother. She died a couple of years ago, from cancer. In fact the kid used to do a lot of charity work. Like read books to dying people . . . that kind of thing. Oh, yeah, once in a while we talked about sports. Boxing mainly. When he was a kid he was a fan of the middleweight champion Marvin Hagler. Sometimes we talked about the Hagler–Hearns fights.

SAM: Did he ever bring a woman in here?

BARTENDER: No. The only one I ever saw him with in here was the captain of the boat he worked on.

SAM: Did he ever talk about his ambitions?

BARTENDER: He was going to law school.

SAM: I'm talking about other kinds of ambitions. Money. Women. Fame. Travel. You know, stuff like that.

BARTENDER: Maybe. I don't remember.

Sam thanked him. The conversation was over. We remained at the bar and drank two steins of draft beer in complete silence. No one came in or out of the place. I had the sense that we were all frozen in time. Four drunks, one bartender, Sam and me.

When the bartender moved down to the other end of the bar, Sam spoke two words to me: "He's lying."

"The bartender, you mean? About what?"

"About the kid."

"How do you know that? He seemed very straightforward and honest to me. He says he only spoke to Rupp a few times."

Anger flashed in Sam's eyes. "Look, honey, no one can read bartenders like me. It's what I do for a living."

I knew better than to argue. "Okay, he lied. So what do we do next?"

"You got any cash on you?"

"Some. Why do you ask?"

"Spring for a cab back to the city, doll. I'm beat."

"That's an excellent idea. We can continue this part of our investigation some other time."

It took an hour to find a cab in Sheepshead Bay that was not only available but willing to go to Manhattan.

Close to midnight, I was back in my loft, exhausted.

The light on the answering machine was blinking but I ignored it. I fed Bushy and Pancho with loving care. I even gave Pancho his most sought-after dessert: a few spoonfuls of saffron rice in his special blue bowl.

I find Portuguese art songs quite soothing, so I put on a CD by the fascinating Cesaria Evora. Then I crawled into bed, fully clothed, and lay there dumbly.

After eating, the cats joined me on the bed. I suddenly felt very good; it had been a long time since we'd had one of these sessions. Bushy, the Maine coon, was standing up straight, primping and prancing and waiting to be groomed. The old boy loved to look good.

Pancho, on the other hand, was at the furthest reaches of the bed, crouched low, suspicious, as always ready to bolt.

We had one of our discussions. Were they getting along? Did they feel all right? What did they think of the chow they were getting these days? I always spoke to them in a nonpatronizing tone. They would either yawn or glare or wash themselves in response, and sometimes I could decipher it—not often, though. Anyway, what did it matter? They were feline, I human. And never the twain would meet, which was absolutely perfect and absolutely mysterious.

The *fado* songs stopped. The cats grew weary of our conversation and took off. Then I got off the bed and listened to my messages. One was from Tony—he sounded drunk and he was reciting a Gerard Manley Hopkins poem.

The second message was from Les Rawls, who spoke very quietly and intently. He wanted to know when he would see me again . . . when I would spend the night with him again. I could hear the urgency in his voice. It was palpable. I felt a sudden rush of the same urgency; I wished I was with him at that moment. It was beyond desire, I realized. I needed the man now.

I took a shower, had a cup of tea and a small cheese sandwich. By that time I was not tired at all. I prowled around the apartment, straightening things, leafing through books, re-indexing my CD collection.

The apartment was becoming frigid. I put on a few sweaters and crawled back into bed with a mystery novel featuring a jazz pianist who investigated the murder of a fellow musician. My friend Nora had passed the book on to me last summer.

It dawned on me as I was reading that poor Calvin Rupp, killed in a futile burst of heroism, could have been the lead character in a mystery novel.

And then, suddenly, lying there enjoying the book, *it* hit me like a ton of bricks.

It being the bartender's comments about how Calvin read to terminally ill patients.

Dying of what? It didn't matter.

Why hadn't I picked up on that before?

The driver of the M14 bus worked part-time at a hospice—a place where people went to die.

The hero of the M8 shooting spent his spare time reading to dying patients.

Connection? Of course there was some kind of connection.

And then I had an even more intense feeling. Maybe it was because of the revelation of a possible connection. I had this absolute certainty that not only were Jerry Bock and Calvin Rupp and the hospice tied together somehow—but an element in that tie was the strange children's book Teresa had obtained from the M8 shooter and never turned in.

No, no! I realized what I really was thinking was that Teresa Positi herself was involved somehow with the bus driver because the transmission of the story to him and his subsequent holding of the information until he finished his run stank to high heaven.

Suddenly I was very warm. I pulled off one of the sweaters, the biggest one. I felt triumphant.

Then I sobered up. Two sides of this triangle were already erased. Calvin and Teresa were dead.

Only the bus driver was alive. And him, I realized, I would have to spook. Bad.

Chapter 13

Believe it or not, the next morning, at around ten, I purchased a frog at the pet store on East 14th Street.

It was a small leopard frog. And with it was a tank, and with the tank, worms.

Why? It seemed intelligent at the time. I wanted to shake, rattle, and roll the bus driver. And I was sure by that time that Teresa Positi and her frog book and her cat food cans were part of some kind of scam, some kind of staged event along with the bus driver. And they were all tied in somehow with Calvin Rupp and the other poor dead people on the M8 bus.

I waited at the bus stop on 14th Street. Six buses passed before I saw the one driven by Jerry Bock arrive. He did not recognize me as I climbed aboard and used my Metrocard.

The bus was practically empty.

I sat down right behind him, separated only

by a partition. Leaning forward, I could see practically his entire body except for his face.

The bus proceeded along.

I leaned forward and said, "Hello! Don't you remember me?"

He looked at me through his mirror.

"No."

"I talked to you in the hospice. About the shooting on the bus."

"Oh, yeah. I remember you now."

"How are you doing?"

"Fine."

"I forgot to ask you—were you close to Calvin Rupp?"

"The name's not familiar. Never heard of him."

"Sure you have, Jerry. He was killed on the M8. He used to volunteer at the same hospice where you work. He would read to the patients."

"I don't know what you're talking about. Why don't you sit back, lady."

I did sit back. I could tell I had unnerved him, though. I let it sink in a bit and then I leaned forward again.

"I did visit Teresa Positi, like you suggested."

"What are you talking about?"

"I went to her apartment."

"She's dead."

"Yes. But I met a friend of hers. You know,

it seems that Teresa didn't tell you everything about the woman in the bus with the gun. And she didn't give you everything the woman dropped. Teresa picked up more than just cat food."

He did not respond. So I got sarcastic.

"And to think that cop, Logan, thought you were just a bus driver who moonlights at a hospice. Isn't that funny?"

He didn't answer. But I could feel the tension emanating from his body. I could feel his foot and hand become heavy in steering the bus.

I let it soak in some more.

Then I leaned forward and said in a laughing mode: "It's really all too complex for me. I mean, all these people running around. All these strange connections, hints, innuendoes, possible conspiracies. Don't you think it's very complex, Jerry?"

"Shut up, lady! Let me drive the bus."

"Tell me, Jerry. You knew Teresa Positi. How well? You knew Calvin Rupp. How well? Did you also know the woman who supposedly pointed a gun on the M14? Did you know the driver of the M8? Did you know the shooter on the M8 bus? Jerry, I believe you are the wisest man in the entire transit system."

He didn't say a word.

"Why don't you just tell me the truth, Jerry? You'll feel a lot better."

He didn't respond.

I leaned back and closed my eyes. This wasn't going very well.

So I played my trump card.

I stood up and walked over to him holding the small cardboard box that was the carrier for my newly purchased $37.50 frog. I could feel my new friend bouncing around in the box, somewhat angrily.

I moved right next to Jerry; actually, I was looking down on the seated figure of the bus driver.

"Get the hell away from me. Get away from the driver. Stand behind the white line."

I hesitated. The thought came to me that I had gone off on one of the wildest wild-goose chases of my life. I had grafted a whole bunch of disparate information . . . some of it, like the frog-and-toad book, totally meaningless and unconnected . . . and come up with a frothing brew.

But, for whatever reason, most likely my new-found success in work and love, I could not be stopped.

I said to the driver, "Teresa gave me a gift, you know."

"I'm warning you! Stay behind the line."

I sensed that he had slowed the bus down considerably and we were not near a bus stop.

"Don't you want to see what's in the box?"

I shoved it under his nose and opened it.

To my astonishment, the frog jumped out with an enormous leap and landed on the windshield.

Jerry swerved toward the curb and stopped the bus. The doors opened.

I was thrown backward. The frog started leaping around crazily. I recovered and ran after it.

Then came an incredible concatenation of events.

Something pulled at my arm. I swung my bag around and felt it hit something. I heard a thud and turned around.

A police officer was lying on the floor. Two standing uniformed officers were right behind him. It seemed that the driver had signaled a dispatcher that there was trouble on the bus.

I was handcuffed, arrested, and booked. There were two charges: creating a public nuisance and assaulting a police officer.

Seven hours later I was released on my own recognizance from the precinct at 19th Street.

Nessem was outside to greet me. He did not beat around the bush. He handed me all my personal possessions, including the frog, and told me that I was terminated as a RETRO consultant; that he did not wish to see me in the office at all; that the things I'd left at the office would be sent to me along with a check for the entire six-week contract.

It was bye-bye, Cat Woman.

*　　*　　*

Breakfast with Sam on Hudson Street at my request. He didn't know what had happened. I enlightened him.

"You just ruined my appetite," he said.

"Do I look crazy, Sam?"

"No. But you sure acted like a nutcase."

We both ordered bacon and eggs. We both didn't say a word until the food arrived. We both didn't pick up a fork.

"A nervous breakdown, probably," he noted.

"Probably."

"You had a lot on your plate, honey. It overwhelmed you. It's for the best. Losing a job is always for the best."

I suddenly burst out: "I can't believe I did what I did."

"You mean the frog?"

"Yes. Can you imagine it? I go to a store and buy a frog and shove it under a bus driver's nose. What was I thinking?"

"You tell me. I mean, honey, I can understand how a sane person would inflate a fact into something relevant. Rupp did read to dying patients, or so that bartender said. And most dying patients, if they're not at home, are in hospitals or hospices. And the driver did moonlight for a hospice. And both men are somehow connected to crimes that may be connected. It's a stretch, but a sane person can arrive at that point. The frog bit? That's another kettle of fish. You just broke down. Overloaded. You were looking for something, anything, to pull yourself up and out. You made up a fairy tale and you believed it. Hey! Aren't frogs and toads often in fairy tales?"

"You think I ought to get help, Sam?"

"You mean a shrink?"

"Yes."

"I don't know. I can't give anybody any advice on that. But I think you should go away for a while. Take a rest. Take a break. Get into a car with this new guy you're seeing and head north or west. I'll take care of your cats."

"That's not a bad idea, Sam."

Suddenly we were both able to eat. We demolished our respective bacon and eggs.

Over coffee I asked: "Will you really look after Bushy and Pancho if Lester and I go away for a while?"

"Yeah, sure."

"And the frog too, Sam?"

"You still have that thing?"

"Yes, of course. He's at the loft. I fixed him up with a nice tank, but I have to keep the lid on so the cats don't get to him."

"Look! I got a great idea. I'll watch the cats and for payment you can give me the frog."

"I didn't know you liked frogs."

"I don't. But I can sell him and make some money."

"Sam, get real. The frog cost me thirty-seven dollars, if I remember right. And there are no pawn shops that will take him."

"No. You don't understand. I'll tell people he's a rare frog from the Amazon rain forest. I read a piece in a science magazine that a lot of companies are sending scientists to the Amazon to collect frogs. It seems that not only do they taste good but the natives chew their bladders to get high. Or something like that. They're full of hallucinogens."

"Are you serious?"

"Of course not."

I felt a whole lot better after that breakfast.

"Are you sad, Alice?"

It was three o'clock in the morning. Lester and I had just finished making love, in his bed, in his apartment.

We were lying on top of the quilt. My head was on his chest. He was playing with my hair. We were warm from the heat of our exertion, even in the frigid room. Inexplicably, his apartment no longer had radiator service.

"No. I'm quite happy about us," I replied.

"I mean about losing the job at RETRO."

"Well, yes. It is a place I like."

Then he said, menacingly, "I will get you another place."

I realized he had purposefully slipped into the mob-lawyer dialect he uses for the *Mulberry Street* series. I slipped into my old gun-moll voice and soon we were having the most ridiculous dialogue in the world.

After we exhausted our script and our bodies became cooler, we crawled under the quilt and began to make plans for our vacation.

"How long you figure us to be away?" he asked.

"I don't think I can impose on Sam for more than a week."

"And we're going north?"

"Right. In a rented car. You and me."

"And we'll stop off to see my people on the Cape?"

"Yes, of course."

"And then where?"

"North."

"But where?"

"Maybe to Vermont, to see some cows."

"It's winter, Alice. The cows are in barns."

"So what?"

"Where will we be sleeping? Inns?"

"Maybe. Maybe roadside motels. Cheap ones, with old TVs and no soap. Or maybe those hotels in small towns. You know the ones I mean: second-floor places with the rooms over hardware stores that look down on Main Street. I always found them romantic."

Les found that funny. He pulled me closer to him.

"And maybe Maine, after that. I think I've been to Maine only twice in my life."

"You do realize it'll be very cold in Maine."

I was about to assure him that he wouldn't be cold when his telephone rang.

Les looked at me and shrugged in a gesture that meant he couldn't imagine who would be phoning him at this time of night.

He picked up the phone from the small table next to the bed. He listened for a bit. Then he looked at me and mouthed the word *Tony*. Lester placed his hand over the receiver. "Did you give him this number?"

"No."

He handed me the phone.

"What the hell are you doing there, Swede?"

"Forget that question, Tony. What do you mean by calling me at this hour?"

"I'm inviting you to a party."

"I'm not interested."

"Listen, reconsider. This is going to be a wonderful party. Believe me."

There was something odd about the way he was talking. Something very odd . . . halfway between a threat and a sexual proposition.

"I mean," he continued, "it may not be as

much fun as the party you've been having there all night, but the hosts here are nicer. We have two lovely cats in charge of the food and drink and a frog who's a most charming fellow."

I covered the phone, suddenly frightened. "He's in my apartment," I whispered to Lester.

My apartment! What was he doing there? How dared he!

All kinds of things were going through my head. Because I know Tony often had his problems with my cats. Maybe he had flipped. Maybe he was merely high. Maybe he was ugly drunk. Maybe he intended to exact some awful vengeance from those animals for crimes he believed I had visited upon him—like abandonment.

I remembered his crazy look . . . making faces through that barroom window at me and Sam. And then for some reason I had that flash of memory—the young woman in the bus stairwell, her weapon belching death.

I said quickly into the phone: "Yes, I'll come to your party, Tony." And I hung up. "I have to get over there fast," I told Les.

"Didn't you take your key back from him?"

"No. It never dawned on me I needed to."

"I think I should go with you."

"No. If he is crazy, your presence will make him crazier."

I dressed quickly and rushed downstairs with

Lester. It's funny how easy it is to get a cab on a freezing street at 3:30 A.M. in New York—if you're white and female.

I kissed Les good-bye, promised to keep him informed of my every move, and was at the front door of my loft building in fifteen minutes—a record cab trip, since there were no other cars around and the lights seemed to align themselves with my vehicle's needs. Or was that just my imagination?

I rang the bell to let him know I was coming up and then climbed the stairs.

The door was open for me.

Bushy gave out a huge meow. I saw a glowering Pancho on the widowsill.

"Tony!" I called out. Where the hell was he?

Then I found him. He must have been terribly drunk. He was sitting on the floor, his back against the wall.

I walked over to him, furious. But then I saw he was not drunk, or if he was, it didn't matter, because the reason he was on the floor in that strange position was because there was a knife plunged deep into the right side of his stomach.

Chapter 14

Sam and I waited outside the hospital room. The police were inside with Tony. The doctors said he would survive. The blade missed vital organs. There was a great deal of shock and blood loss, but all that could be remedied.

I no longer had any idea what time it was, but it had to be some time in the morning.

"Stop pacing, Nestleton. Sit down. Relax."

I nodded to Sam that I would do as he said, but I just kept moving and fretting. I blamed myself for this mess. Who else was there to blame? Not for the robbery, of course, but for Tony's dementia. Obviously it was my affair with Lester Rawls that had sent him around the bend, driven him to occupy my loft.

The police came out. Sam and I went in.

My legs grew weak when I saw him, lying in that bed, so pale, so wan, so still. His thick hair was matted and he looked as though he had shed twenty pounds in a few hours.

He saw us. He raised one hand feebly. I rushed to the bed, grabbed his hand, and kissed it.

"Calm down, Swede," he whispered. "I'm really not interested in sex now."

Sam found that very funny.

I sat down on the bed beside him, still holding his hand.

Sam hovered nearby, inspecting the various hospital utensils, like glass drinking straws.

"I'm sorry about this mess," Tony said.

"Be quiet, Tony. You rest now."

"Do you really love that guy, Swede?"

I didn't know how to respond. I played with a sheet. This was all so sad and bizarre.

"I just wanted to see you, Swede . . . to be with you."

"I understand, Tony."

"Things have not been going so good."

"Yes, I know. Why don't you sleep for a while."

"She knifed me."

"What?"

"It was a woman."

"You mean the thief?"

"Yes. I didn't see her face. And I was drunk. I was waiting for you to come home. And I was stumbling around the loft and I heard someone enter, Swede. I thought it was you. But I had turned all the lights out. Romantic stuff, see."

Tony was breathing hard now, and obviously in pain, but he wouldn't stop talking.

"All of a sudden, Swede, the thing went into me. God, it hurt. I grabbed it. I felt my own blood squishing out. And then I grabbed her. I didn't see her face. She was big. But I know it was a woman—a light-haired, big woman. Because I grabbed for her chest and I felt breasts— a woman's breasts."

"All right, Tony. I believe you."

"Call the nurse, Swede. Get me something. My stomach hurts like hell."

I squeezed the button to get the nurse.

Tony closed his eyes and his hand gripped mine very hard.

"She'll be here in a minute, Tony."

"That guy isn't for you, Swede."

"Okay."

"You really do hate it when I call you Swede, don't you? You've always hated it."

"Forget about that right now."

"You don't want to spend the rest of your life with an actor."

"No, I don't."

And then the nurse came in. Sam and I eased ourselves out of the room. We walked down the hall.

"I have to get back to the loft, Sam. I have to make sure the cats are all right, see what kind of damage was done to the place."

"Do you think he was delusional, Nestleton?"

"About what?"

"The intruder."

"No, I don't."

"He could be lying. It could have been some guy who had a beef with him. Maybe he seduced some tough guy's girlfriend and the guy decided she'd be the last one Basillio ever did. And now he's too ashamed to admit it."

"No, I believe him."

We walked all the way back to my loft and climbed the stairs slowly.

Except for the dried blood on the floor, the loft was in fairly good shape. Obviously someone had gone through it looking for valuables, but nothing seemed to be missing.

As for Bushy and Pancho, they seemed in excellent shape. In fact, the commotion seemed to have energized them. They gulped their food and then started prowling, as if looking for more mayhem.

Sam asked, a bit nastily, "Are you going to interrogate them, Cat Woman?"

"Not right now," I replied.

Then Sam saw the tank. "Is that the beast?" he asked.

"That's him."

He walked over to the tank and inspected the frog, who was seated calmly on a tiny fake log covered with plastic moss.

"He looks pretty smart," Sam noted.

"Couldn't prove it by me. Feed him some of the dried worms."

While Sam did just that, I continued my perusal of the apartment. I found bank checks and my passport. I found my jewelry, what there was of it, including the heirlooms from my grandmother.

"Looks like nothing was taken."

"Maybe they busted into the wrong apartment," Sam offered. "You got some kind of photographer on the floor below, don't you?"

"That's right."

"There you go. That's probably where they meant to break in. A lot of expensive equipment lying around. Or maybe a photograph that should never see the light of day."

He sat down on the sofa and rested. The cats joined him, to my surprise.

I called Lester and told him everything was all right. For some reason I didn't want to tell him that Tony had been stabbed, or even that the apartment had been broken into.

Then I sat down beside Sam. Bushy immediately jumped into my lap.

From where we sat I could see the blood on the floor.

"You have any coffee, honey? I'll take that instant espresso you like."

"Kitchen counter," I answered.

"You got any brandy?"

"Yes."

"What about some sweet cream?"

"No. But I think there's half-and-half in the refrigerator."

"Nestleton, I'm gong to prepare one of my specialties, intended for morning crises."

I waved him into the kitchen. Let him do whatever he wanted.

In a short while he brought back an astonishing brew: a mixture of far too strong Medaglia d'Oro doused with far too much sugar and half-and-half, and way too much cheap brandy (the only kind I had).

But I had to give the old reprobate credit; after a few sips the loft and my situation and the world looked considerably better.

"I hope," Sam said, "you're not going to postpone your vacation."

"I don't know."

"Tony will be fine."

"Probably."

"You really gotta get away, Nestleton. Too many bad things happening."

"We were thinking of going up to Maine."

"Sounds nice, if that's your idea of a good time."

"And you'll still watch the cats for me."

"Sure I will. I'm looking forward to it. And the frog, honey . . . the frog, too."

"Okay."

"By the way, what's the frog's name?"

"I don't know."

"He needs a name, Nestleton."

"Fine. Give him one."

"How about Ruthie? Just in case it's really a lady frog."

"Fine."

"Oh, yeah. What does he eat besides worms?"

"I don't know, Sam. Go to the pet store where I bought him. The one on 14th Street. Or read all about it in that frog-and-toad book I showed you."

"Good idea. Where is it?"

"In my other bag, by the phone."

He went to the bag and began to rummage.

"Not here," he said.

"Really? I'm sure I didn't take it out. But check the shelf there."

He searched the bookshelf. Nothing. I searched every tote bag and purse I owned. We looked all around, but the book never turned up.

I felt addled. "Do you think it's possible, Sam? What I'm thinking—you think it's credible?"

"What's that?"

"That Tony was nearly killed by a woman who broke in here just to steal a book about frogs and toads."

Tully and I looked at each other.

"If I'm right about that, Sam, the break-in and the assault on Tony are part of the ongoing investigation."

"Or it means that after RETRO fired you, you abandoned your Cat Woman status and needed some ego boost. So, voila, you become Frog Woman."

I held up my hand to shush him. Something very elementary had popped into my befuddled head. "Sam, do you remember the description Tony gave of his assailant?"

"Yeah . . ."

"It could well have been a description of Natasha Whatshername."

"Who?"

"One of the people shot on the M8 bus."

"Isn't she still in the hospital?"

"I don't know."

"But she was hurt bad, wasn't she?"

"Yes."

"So how is she going to climb stairs, break into a place, and drive a knife into Basillio's gut like that? And I mean drive it deep in."

"You're right, I guess."

"Be cool, honey. Just because that book is missing, you can't jump to conclusions. Hey, get it? I made a pun. The book's about frogs, right? Frogs? Jumping?"

"Very witty."

"How do you know you didn't just leave that stupid book somewhere? Let's face it, you've been moving around quite a bit lately. And sleeping in a strange bed or two, no?"

"Have I really been doing that, Sam? 'Sleeping around.' At my age?"

He actually began to speculate on that issue.

I wasn't listening to him. I was imagining the woman who had knifed Tony so viciously. Sam was absolutely right. No matter how close the description, Natasha was incapable of such a feat given her medical condition. There was also the possibility that Tony didn't know what he was talking about. He was in the apartment in the wee hours of the morning with all the lights off, drunk, crazed with jealousy. That description might have been a delusion, as Sam had suggested.

Still, he didn't knife himself.

Sam babbled on. Now he seemed to be extolling the virtues of promiscuity among older women. He got up and made himself another Tully cocktail.

Something was happening to my face, I realized . . . a twitch. It felt awfully strange.

I walked over to the one large mirror and looked at myself.

I was shabbily dressed. Flannel slacks and a threadbare sweater of indeterminate color. A thick wool band held my hair off my face. Wrists bared because the old sweater's sleeves were too short, I looked like a scarecrow.

But my face, I had to admit, was wonderful. I was smiling.

Pancho zoomed between my legs on one of his mad dashes, his half-tail held up in the air, his ears flattened back against his head, his gray coat as dull as a scuttled warship.

"You're still a knockout, honey," I heard Sam say.

It was only then that I realized why I was smiling: There was another woman who fit the description Tony gave us.

I stared at my smiling face. Smile on.

The dominos were beginning to fall.

I turned to Sam.

"Care to go for a drive with me?" I asked him.

"You got wheels?"

"I got a credit card."

Chapter 15

We were seated in a rented car, double-parked across the street from the Sun Hospice.

Sam was behind the wheel. I was in the passenger seat holding a small cardboard box that functioned as the frog carrier. I could hear Ruthie inside, grumbling or whatever it is that frogs do when unhappy.

"I hope you remember, honey, that the last tine you freed Ruthie you got arrested and fired."

"I am aware of that. But this time you are going to be the one who frees him."

"I'm overjoyed."

"It'll take only a minute, Sam. Just use the brass knocker. You'll be buzzed in. Then, the minute you get inside, let Ruthie out. Then you walk out, close the door behind you, and come back to the car. Don't tarry."

"And the point of all this is . . . ?"

"Panic."

"Like letting loose a mouse in a girls' shower room."

"Close. But not quite."

Sam looked at me as if I were mad, and I understood why. He sighed, took the box with Ruthie in it, and exited the vehicle.

I saw him swing the brass knocker.

I saw him enter the hospice.

And I saw him leave.

He returned to our rented car.

"Okay. What next?"

"We wait," I said.

"Isn't this the place where your bus driver moonlights?"

"Yes. But we're not waiting for Jerry."

"Then who?"

"Lila Gibbons."

"And who might that be?"

"An employee of the Sun Hospice. A heavyset blondish woman who may have put that knife in poor Basillio."

"How long do we wait?"

I shrugged.

"And what if she does come out? What do you want to do?"

"Follow her."

"And I assume, Nestleton, that you think dropping poor Ruthie in there is going to spook her somehow."

"That's it, Sam."

"Of course, she might just pick up a broom and whack him."

I didn't reply.

"You are a piece of work, honey."

"Well, thank you, Sam."

He opened the driver's-side window and lit a cigarette. I tried to keep warm. But maybe I was shivering from excitement . . . from the chase. Or maybe from fear that the frog ploy was absurd, the way the first one had been.

Lila Gibbons emerged twenty minutes later. She wore a wool hat pulled down over her ears.

She entered an old green Volvo station wagon parked near the corner, started the engine, and drove off.

We followed the Volvo.

She drove to a Citibank on Broadway near 85th Street, parked precariously and illegally, and went inside. She spent some twenty minutes there.

Then she drove to Columbus Avenue, parked, and went into an HSBC branch. Ten minutes there.

When she came out she made a phone call from a street booth.

Then she drove to a Chase Bank on Broadway at 110th. She was in there a long time.

"What do you think is going on in these banks?" I asked Sam.

"What do you do at any bank? She's either putting money in or taking it out."

"But she's carrying nothing going in and nothing coming out."

"Yeah. You're right."

"And the banks aren't crowded. Obviously she isn't just dealing with tellers. What about a loan officer, Sam?"

"Maybe. But it might be safe deposit boxes. Taking out jewelry or something like that. But, like you said, she's not carrying anything."

"What about cash?"

"Which she converts to cashier's checks? Maybe."

He lit another cigarette and started mumbling: "I know Ruthie is ugly and slimy, but how the hell could he spook a grown woman into a bank withdrawal frenzy? And how could a hospice employee have safe deposit boxes or accounts in all these banks? No. No. We don't know what's going on. Maybe nothing's going on."

We waited in silence for a while, the tension rising.

She exited the bank and made another call on a public phone. She seemed to be angry now, yelling at the person on the other end of the line.

"Why don't you tell me everything you know about this lunacy, Nestleton. I mean, it looks like I'm your permanent chauffeur now."

I pointed my finger at the woman by the phone booth. "She's the one who knows, Sam.

I'm as dumb as you. I'm feeling around in the dark. All I know is that she's afraid of frogs."

It was a gentle, necessary lie wrapped in a truth.

"Wait a minute, Nestleton. You're being cute. You know a whole lot more than that. Like she may hate Tony enough to want to kill him. And—"

The conversation was aborted because the woman had slammed the phone down and was rushing to her car.

She drove off fast. We followed.

First onto the West Side Highway. Then over the George Washington Bridge to New Jersey. Then north on 9W.

The moment she got onto 9W, she slowed down considerably.

The route was an ugly one, gas stations and stores and drive-ins on either side of the highway.

But not far away were dozens of tall residential buildings, many of them obviously of the high-rent variety.

"Where are we?" I asked.

"Fort Lee."

Lila pulled into a gas station, but not to a pump. She parked the car in the rear and used the bathroom.

When she returned, she opened the trunk of

the Volvo and pulled out a large and brightly colored plastic bottle. It was the kind you expect to contain liquid detergent or fabric softener.

"What's she going to do, wash the car?" Sam speculated. Then he added, "Maybe she's a moonshiner."

But she headed away from the vehicle, carrying the plastic bottle, and walked to a narrow dirt road north of the gas station, which ran in an east–west direction, connecting to 9W.

"Maybe she's heading for her still," Tully quipped.

We exited our vehicle and followed her on foot, west, away from the highway.

There were bare scrub woods on either side.

Lila Gibbons walked down that ugly dirt road for about half a mile. She walked quickly, resolutely, looking neither to the left nor to the right nor behind her. A very light snow was beginning to fall.

Then she turned off the road into a rundown warehouse area.

One of the buildings contained a mini storage facility. It was simply an amalgam of rental bins . . . some the size of a garage, some much smaller. Each one had a lock on the door of the bin, which faced out.

She fiddled with the lock of a medium-sized bin. Sam and I insinuated ourselves in the shadows of the building.

When she got the door open, she placed the large plastic bottle on the ground just outside the door. She removed an old-fashioned straw broom from the bin and stood it next to the bottle.

"A long chase to watch a cleaning lady," Sam whispered nastily.

Then Lila Gibbons removed a large black plastic garbage bag and carried it to a nearby Dumpster.

She went back and forth between the bin and the Dumpster twice more with bags similar to the first one. They did not appear easy to carry.

Then she laid the broom on the ground and poured some liquid from the bottle onto the broom head.

"She's going to do a serious cleaning," Sam noted.

And then a very strange thing happened.

She didn't go into the bin this time. She headed back to the Dumpster carrying only the broom.

It was only when she knelt next to the Dumpster, shielded herself from the wind, lit a match, and applied it to the broom head that I realized the bags contained evidence and it was about to be destroyed.

She flung the fiercely burning broom into the Dumpster.

I started to run toward it.

Sam was yelling out to me to stop, but I didn't stop.

I ran past a startled Lila Gibbons and climbed up the side of the Dumpster.

Everything inside it was burning and sparking. I grabbed the side of one bag and pulled at it with all my strength.

The burning bag and I fell backward onto the ground.

Sam began to stomp at the fire.

I stood up, unsteady. I saw Lila running toward a car that had suddenly appeared.

A man was standing outside the car next to the open door. He looked vaguely familiar.

Something in his hand began to spit fire.

Sam screamed and fell onto the remains of the plastic bag.

I saw blood pumping out of his thigh.

I dove behind the Dumpster, found my cell phone. My fingers were trembling so badly it took me three attempts to call 911.

I peered out. Lila and the man and the car and the gun had vanished.

I rushed to Sam, crouched beside him and tried to stop the bleeding with my sweater. He was groaning and rolling his head around.

Some small singed boxes had fallen out of the burnt trash bag.

Inside the boxes were what appeared to be

oversized pills, gray in color with an oblong shape.

There was something printed on each box.

I kicked the closest one with my foot so I could read it. The blood from Sam's leg had immediately soaked through my sweater.

STOMACH EXTRACT / FOWLER'S TOAD

That's what the box read. And in smaller type: 20 TABLETS.

Chapter 16

It was some twenty-four hours later that the phone call came in from Nessem of RETRO. The time was around four in the afternoon.

I had spent the previous night with Sam in a Fort Lee hospital. He was doing fine, considering his injuries, age, and lifestyle.

And I had spent the morning with Tony in his hospital room. He was doing fine too, given his stomach wound and his state of mind.

Lester had been calling all day and leaving desperate messages. I didn't pick up the phone. I didn't return his calls.

Sure, I understood that he was worried. But the events of the past two days—the horror of it all—had somehow transformed my lover into a kind of footnote.

Yes, I know it's strange and it may say something about me that is not very nice. But he now seemed small and far away.

When the call from Nessem came in, I was

lying on my bed, drifting in and out of sleep. I was drained, bone weary, confused, sick with worry over Sam and Tony.

Why did I pick up when I heard Nessem's voice on the machine?

I don't know, but I did pick up.

"Did you hear?" he asked.

"What?"

"We got them."

"Got who?"

"They were in a motel in Ellenville . . . upstate. The woman and the bus driver. With $750,000 in cashier's checks. Halleck went up there. The bus driver cracked like a soft-boiled egg. How in God's name did you figure it out?"

I didn't reply. What had I figured out, really? I surmised from Tony's description of his assailant that she might be Lila Gibbons. And I knew from my search of my apartment that whoever had attacked him had stolen the frog-and-toad book. I had melded these facts with Sam's joking comment about how valuable certain frogs and toads were because of their chemical properties. So I had released poor Ruthie operating on the assumption that something about frogs and toads was crucial to what was happening—and the release would spook Lila Gibbons.

It had worked beyond my wildest dreams.

But what did I really know?

"Look," Nessem said, "I want to see you. I'm

sending my car around to your place at around seven. The driver will ring the buzzer."

"Don't you remember that you fired me?"

"I think, Alice Nestleton, you owe it to those people who took hits for you to know the final resolution of the case."

I cursed him and hung up.

But when the buzzer rang at seven, I was dressed and ready to go.

Alas, I was dressed a bit too informally for where I was taken by the NYPD driver. To Forlini's, the pub on Baxter Street that was the preferred watering hole of judges, lawyers, and highly placed cops.

Nessem was waiting. He greeted me as if I was Cleopatra disembarking from a Roman ship, as if I was queen of the Nile, and he led me to a table where the champagne was already on ice.

He poured and toasted me.

"You were brilliant, Cat Woman. Even that first frog idiocy on the bus was spectacular—in retrospect, that is. It did nothing but get you arrested at the time, but you had stumbled on the right track. You were making the connections."

"What did the bus driver tell Halleck?"

"Everything. It was just an old-fashioned patent medicine scam that got out of control. Lila Gibbons conducted interviews with people who wanted their dying relatives to be cared for in a hospice. She would select one of these individuals and tell him or her that maybe no hospice care was needed, maybe the loved one would recover at home. How? Lila had access to a new experimental drug extracted from the stomachs of Fowler's toads, a rare Amazonian creature. Scientists who were testing it believed it was a wonder drug, particularly for cancer. Of course, everything was a lie. The Fowler's toad does not come from the Amazon. It is a common North American amphibian. Its stomach lining has no miraculous properties. There was no extract at all provided. The pills you found in the Dumpster were sugar pills. By the way, each box of those gray sugar pills costs the grieving relative $2,000."

Nessem paused, smiled, and refilled our glasses. He waited for a response. I had none. He continued.

"Gibbons was smart. The money was paid first. The pills were delivered a few days later. That way, all quid pro quo's were avoided. And the passing of the pills from Gibbons to the mark was always done on an M14 bus that was being driven by Jerry Bock, whom Gibbons had recruited while he was moonlighting at the hospice. Gibbons told the mark to board the bus at a certain time and stand in the back of the bus at a certain place carrying a shopping bag. Then she just dropped the pills into the bag without a word said. Bock's job was to keep watch in his mirror, to make sure the mark was not accompanied by anyone. And to provide a witness in case something went wrong. If Gibbons was picked up, Bock would testify that she was standing in front of the bus near him and could not have dropped the pills into the bag."

"It was ingenious," I noted.

"Yes. But sooner or later someone would realize it was a scam. Someone would see her life savings lost, her loved one dead, and realize that vengeance must be extracted, no matter Gibbons's excuse that the Fowler toad pills did not work every time. That's what happened on the M14 three years ago. But the woman's gun jammed. And there was no vengeance."

The waiter came with menus. I wasn't hungry. Nessem ordered leg of lamb.

He smiled at me.

"You know the rest of the story, don't you?"

"Well, I imagine after that jammed-gun incident, Bock got nervous, so Gibbons transferred the operation to the M8 line."

"Exactly. And everything went smoothly. There were no other vengeance seekers. The marks just swallowed their loss and grief. They probably figured they had gambled on a long shot and lost, not realizing the race was fixed. There was no possibility of a cure because there was no drug but sugar. They even hired a third conspirator—Calvin Rupp—to do the packaging of the fake pills and collect the money. Calvin had been a volunteer at the hospice, reading and entertaining the dying."

He stopped and tapped his fork on the champagne glass. He obviously wanted me to lead now. The champagne was kicking in; I obliged him.

"And then another vengeance seeker arose," I said.

"Yes."

"And boarded my bus."

"Exactly. But Gibbons could not make it that day. She had the flu. Isn't that ridiculously mundane? But it's true. So she sent Calvin Rupp to drop the pills into the shopping bag."

It suddenly dawned on me. "Oh, my God! The woman was so deranged with hatred that she shot at a look-alike."

"Yes. Natasha Larish."

"So when Rupp ran after the shooter, it wasn't for noble reasons, but just to get rid of a loose cannon who could sink them all."

"Exactly," affirmed Nessem.

"Did Bock give you the names of the shooters?"

"Yes. We're looking for them now. But remember, Gibbons and Bock also tried unsuccessfully to hunt them down."

Then he leaned far over the table toward me in a kind of conspiratorial style. He asked: "Do you know how good this case makes RETRO look?"

"Quite good, I imagine."

"Hell! We're the king of the hill now. But just think, if I hadn't assigned you to that old M14 incident, which no one but me and RETRO believed was tied to the M8 murders, nothing would have happened. I mean nothing. You investigated that witness at my urging. You found the deceased witness's friend, who had saved a children's book the shooter with the jammed gun had carried. The book that Gibbons had to get back because it was the only piece of hard data tying the Fowler toad to the whole mess. Oh, yes! RETRO is going to be a big player from now on."

His food came. He leaped on it, but after two impressive bites he put his utensils down. The smell of the lamb was staggering.

"You know the strangest thing about this case?"

"No."

"We hired you because we thought there was a cat connection. But the cans of cat food left by the M14 shooters and the live cat left by the M8 shooter were not related at all. It was just one of those strange coincidences that pop up. They meant nothing. It gets stranger. After we hired you because you were the Cat Woman, you metamorphosed into the Frog Woman."

"I suppose it is strange."

"Anyway, we want you back. And I'm offering a much longer contract and a much more lucrative one."

"I'm not interested."

"Oh, come on! What else do you have to do?"

"I'm an actress."

"But if that series bombs, you'll be out of work. I heard you're the most highly acclaimed, permanently underemployed Off-Broadway actress in the city."

"Look, let me think about your offer."

"Think hard."

I wondered just how much money I could extort from him. I wondered how much I wanted to go back.

He grinned at me, thinking. I wanted to punish him.

"You know," I said, "it was never the capacity of RETRO's computers that intrigued me. Not the first time I was there and not the last time."

"It's the coffee then," he quipped.

"No. Just the sense that here was a group of people working in a small space and their only task was to solve old, cold cases . . . resurrect cases that were dead . . . dig up corpses that had been forgotten . . . do justice where none had existed."

My, I had said a mouthful. He mocked me with: "Act one, scene two, honey?"

It disturbed me that he suddenly sounded like Sam.

I said, "To be honest, I find your Criminal Investigations Database idiotic."

Actually I didn't, but I felt compelled to make such a statement. Sam and Tony were both in the hospital. They were the martyrs. They were the linchpins. They were the detectives in mufti.

He said, "I love beautiful Luddites."

"The fact is," I reminded him, "it was just the random reappearance of a petty childhood disorder in an old woman—theft—that broke this case."

"But, like I said before, it was the CID that got you to that woman who stole the silly book in the first place."

"I would have found her and it sooner or later."

"In police work, Miss Nestleton, 'sooner or later' means impotence. Look, I don't want to argue. I'm giving you and your friends half the credit. And I'm giving RETRO the other half. Don't you get it? We're a team, not unlike Batman and Robin, Oppenheimer and Groves, Nick and Nora, Lunt and Fontaine. You're the woman who finds threads that no one else sees. And I'm the sewing box backing you up."

"Or the litter box."

His eyes narrowed. "What?"

"A joke," I replied, and then added: "I'll think about it and let you know."

Then Nessem proceeded to get drunk from the champagne and started to spin out stories about RETRO, many of which I had heard during my first brief tenure there.

The drunker he got, the happier he became. He was fulfilled. Stern Nessem became bloody ecstatic.

I felt neither joy nor accomplishment.

"I want to go home," I said.

He didn't argue. His driver took me home in the same streamlined Town Car that had brought me.

I collapsed onto the bed, fully clothed.

But I couldn't sleep.

I had the strange feeling that I had crossed a bridge, a barrier, a demarcation line . . . that I had entered a different country.

I put on a very old record, something I hadn't played for years: the Kris Kristofferson album that contained "Me and Bobby McGee." I believe it once belonged to Tony.

I grabbed one of my yellow pads and started one of my signature lists of things to do.

I always did crazy things like that when I was exhausted or sleepless.

It didn't last more than ten minutes, but when the list-making frenzy abated and I studied what I had put down on the yellow pad, I realized it, the list, was quite sane—the sanest thing I had done in a long, long time.

It read:

Send chocolate and flowers to Sam
Find Ruthie, the leopard frog
Quit *Mulberry Street*
Say good-bye to Rawls
Say no to RETRO
Do not ride buses anymore
Take Tony by hand when he leaves hospital and imprison him in my bed and heart
Buy bulk cat litter
Rent rat-infested warehouse in Red Hook, Brooklyn, and do original one-act plays by lunatics and convicts

I read the list over and over and I became happier and happier. I grabbed Bushy and then Pancho and we danced together across the room.

Pancho, in fact, was so overwhelmed by my list that he began to rotate his stump of a tail counterclockwise and make all kinds of significant groans.

Believe it or not, I understood what he was saying. I translated Pancho's comments to Bushy.

He was saying: "Swede, anything is possible!"

What a wise old cat! Of course he had obviously picked up the habit from Tony of calling me something I was not—of Swedish extraction.

But it was a start.

I began to implement my list the next morning.

I arrived at Rawls's apartment at ten-fifteen to say good-bye. He started to shout at me.

"I've been trying to reach you for days. Where the hell have you been? Why didn't you answer my calls?"

I didn't answer.

I walked to his bed and began to undress.

"You're acting crazy, Alice," he said.

But he slipped out of his bathrobe.

We made love with the kind of desperation that usually comes after separation and misunderstanding.

When it was over we lay there silent and exhausted.

"It's a good way to start the day," he noted.

"I won't be seeing you again, Les."

"What?"

I started to dress. I didn't answer.

"Ah," he said bitterly, "I get the strategy. The love-making was in lieu of conversation. You don't want to talk about it—right? Our little thing is over. That's that. You just walk in, make love, tell me, and walk out. You don't take prisoners, Alice Nestleton. Right?"

I walked to the door.

He started to yell: "And you're right, Alice. We're both too old, too hip, too cool to require explanations. When it's over, it's over. When it's broken, it's shattered. It's show biz, Alice. It's Humpty-Dumpty Land. And you're playing the femme fatale."

"Take care of yourself," I said. And then I walked out and took a cab to the hospital.

Tony was propped up in his bed, fast asleep. I sat down on one of the chairs near the bed.

I was upset by my behavior at Lester's place. Why had I behaved so stupidly, so soap opera-ishly? Why had I selected such a hokey scenario—walk in, make love, announce the end, and walk out?

Maybe, I thought, when the pressure is on, my Garbo fantasies emerge and I end up playing a deranged Russian princess.

Poor Les! But he didn't look hurt—just mad.

Tony's eyes opened.

"Are you up?" I asked.

"Yeah."

"Have you been eating?"

"Just liquids."

"Did the doctors say how long you'll be here?"

"Maybe five days."

"Are you in pain?"

"Yeah."

"Are you in pain now?"

"A little. Why?"

"I want to have a conversation with you."

"Sure, Swede. Let's go. I like hearing about your sexual adventures with TV actors."

"Are you capable of fidelity, Tony?"

"What are you talking about?"

"Just think about it for a minute. Think about fidelity. Is it possible for you to be faithful to a person in the same way that you are faithful to the art and craft of stage design?"

"Of course."

"You're sure?"

"Yeah."

"For a year?"

"Yeah. For ten years. You know better than to judge a person by his reputation, Swede."

He reached over and sipped some juice. His lips looked parched.

"Then I have a proposition for you, Tony."

"I'm listening."

"I think it's time we crossed over the bridge."

"You mean get religion?"

"No. I mean geographically."

"Jersey?"

"No. Brooklyn."

"What for?"

"I'm going to tell you."

"You do that, Swede, because given my situation I'm open to all suggestions."

"First, we are going to get back together. We just rid ourselves of all entanglements and get back together. As man and wife."

"Are you serious?"

"Quite serious. But that is only the beginning. We'll take all the money we have left and the cats and move to Greenpoint or Williamsburg or Red Hook. We get settled quick and then we look for a theater."

"A theater? What the hell are you talking about?"

"Space, Tony. A large old warehouse maybe, with plenty of space for your megalomaniacal sets. And we pull in some young actors. And we create a company of players, like the Berliner Ensemble. And we do every crazy script that comes to us."

I shut up. I sat back. I waited.

He took another sip of juice. He started to reply, then was quiet, then readjusted his position in the bed with a grimace and asked, "What about your TV series?"

"I'm out of it."

"What about RETRO?"

"No more."

"What about all the things you do, Swede? The

cat-sitting. The friends. The Off-Off-Broadway stuff. The acting classes."

"Gone!"

"But don't you see what we'll be doing? The same old nonsense. Just recreating us twenty years ago. Coming to the City. Coming to work. Coming to the theater. Looking for something that wasn't there."

"You mean we'll be fools again, Tony?"

"Damn right."

"Well, we paid our dues. We earned the right. Basillio and Nestleton—fools again. And idiots. And demented. Pile it on."

"And you really want us to get married?"

"As fast as possible. All you have to do is keep away from twenty-year-old actresses. You can do it, Tony. You stopped smoking, didn't you?"

He pointed at me menacingly. "No one loves you like I do."

"So you're agreed."

"Of course."

"We'll be married when you're released. Maybe in that Swedish Lutheran church in Murray Hill."

"But you're not Swedish."

"Neither are you," I replied, and then sat down on his bed and kissed him on the eyes.

"You look beautiful, Swede. Like you used to look after we made love."

Then I called a private cab to take me to New Jersey.

I entered Sam's hospital room with flowers and candy. There were three other patients in the large room.

Poor Sam was tied to a chair by his bed.

"Dump that junk and get over here," he called out hoarsely. His thigh was heavily bandaged and his hospital robe was all ripped up.

I put the objects on the windowsill and sat on his bed. It was shocking to see him tied up like that.

"What's going on?" I asked.

"They say the painkillers made me crazy. They say I wouldn't stay in bed; that I was hopping around the hospital making trouble. So they tied me up."

"Maybe we ought to change hospitals, Sam."

"Forget it. Talk, honey. Talk to me."

I told him everything that Nessem had told me. The scam. The bus incidents. The conspirators. The denouement. Everything. He absorbed it all silently.

When I finished, he said, "So it was the bus driver who shot me."

"Yes."

"Do you have a cigarette?"

"No."

"And Nessem wants you back."

"Yes."

"What will he pay this time around?"

"A whole lot more. But the Cat Woman is retiring, Sam."

"To do what?"

"Improvise."

"Well, you did good, doll. Real good."

"Maybe, but it was you, Sam, who loosened all the screws. You were the one who told me to focus on the dead hero, Rupp. And you were the one who told me about frogs and toads with chemical factories in their skin. Sure, you said it was a joke—but it was that joke that got me thinking. It was that joke that led to us releasing Ruthie at the hospice. The rest, as they say, is history."

He grimaced.

"Let's not get too proud, honey. When push comes to shove, it was Nessem who has to get the MVP. It was Nessem who looked at a couple of cans of cat food left on one bus and a cat in a carrier left on another bus—three years apart—and said to himself 'Where is Alice Nestleton now?'

"Of course, it turned out the cat connection didn't mean a damn thing. But so what?"

"I suppose you're right."

"Did you find Ruthie?"

"Not yet."

"Will you feed Pickles for me?"

"Yes."

"Will you go downstairs and get me some cigarettes?"

"No."

He started to fight his restraints but gave up quickly. He closed his eyes. I just sat there. I had the urge to comb his rumpled white hair. But I didn't. The other patients in the room were looking at us with sympathy.

I lay down and fell fast asleep on the hospital bed.

I was awakened by some violent kicks to the bed frame, administered by Sam with his one good leg.

"Listen, honey, I just thought of something."

"I'm listening, Sam."

I sat up, wondering how long I had napped.

"You remember that old fairy tale about the frog who's turned into a prince?"

"Sure."

"Well, how about this? I think I just invented a whole new genre of mystery novel—the Inverted Fairy Tale Whodunit. Here's the way it works. There's this ugly old frog. He's hanging out in a Dumpster behind the Martin Beck Theatre. And one day a beautiful young actress from Minnesota staggers out the back door, weeping and wailing after screwing up an audition for another revival of *Midsummer Night's Dream*.

"She sees the frog. She picks him up and in a fit of compassion kisses him on his abominable face. Presto! The frog is turned immediately into the hard-boiled private eye, Harry Bondo. And then this P.I. and this actress go out into the world of criminal investigation together. But Harry Bondo is a nutcase, so every time he becomes too difficult, our heroine just spits in his right eye and he's turned right back into a frog and she keeps him in her purse until he's needed again."

"Brilliant, Sam."

"Yeah, I agree. Okay. Bring me that candy and pop a few into my mouth. Then get out of here. I have to plot my escape."

I did as I was ordered. As I was exiting, he called out: "Hey!"

"Yes?"

"Remember. Before you do anything, you gotta get back on the M8 bus."

He was so right. There was a good chance the Eileen Fisher winter sale was not over yet.

Please read on for an excerpt
from the previous Alice Nestleton mystery
A Cat Named Brat
Available Now from Signet

How hot was that August night? So hot that even with both loft ceiling fans going at high speed and all my large windows wide open I had to abandon my bed and seek cooler space on the floor, using a terrycloth towel as a sleeping mat.

I was, by then, totally naked. And this, for some reason, unnerved Pancho a bit; he ceased his all-weather pursuit of nonexistent enemies. In fact, my stubby-tailed, dim-witted gray cat just stared at me as if I were a total stranger. Bushy, my Maine coon cat, would have been more sophisticated. But he was staying overnight at the vet, getting his nails done, his health examined, and his attitude adjusted.

It had been so far a slow, constricting, jobless, loveless summer. And it was not over yet. Most of my friends had vanished. Nora was once again taking her vacation on Martha's Vineyard. Tony Basillio was in Los Angeles, looking, he said, for work. Chuckle, chuckle. A.G. Roth, believe it or not, had gone to England for his long-awaited opportunity to make, as he put it, on-the-scene, hard-hitting inquiries concerning the British Secret Service's role in the assassination of Abraham Lincoln. His obsession with this case seemed not only to be ballooning, but now was a full-blown psychosis that in my opinion required hospitalization. I have heard that lawyers are particularly prone to this sort of thing.

The only one of my "circle" not away from the city was Sam Tully, but he was incommunicado, unless you met him in a bar. And that I refused to do in the summer. In hot weather any type of alcohol makes me sick. I can't even stand to be around the stuff. Of course in fall and winter, and even spring, I'm a bit more tolerant.

I had been reading a lot, particularly Henry James. I had always disliked his novels and could never finish a single one. But I had recently found at the Strand a collection of his tales, and they were mesmerizing. Perhaps it was the heat. Anyway, while waiting or looking for jobs, either cat related or theater related, I would read Henry James in spurts.

So that is the way my summer was going—a little of this and a little of that.

That is, until the phone call on that hot night while I was lying nude on the floor.

Usually, when one is naked on the floor at

eleven o'clock on a very hot and sultry summer evening, one expects some kind of romantic thing.

The voice, however, was very prosaic. So was our conversation.

"Is this Alice Nestleton?"

"Yes. Who is this?"

"You don't know me. My name is Louis Montag. I need a cat-sitter, and you were recommended to me."

"By whom?"

"By a man in a bar. I think his name was Samuel."

Uh-oh, I thought. If this Montag was drinking in the same bar that Sam was, it had to be a seedy, ugly bar. Did I really want to have a business arrangement with him? Any kind of arrangement? But he did sound rather normal.

He waited for me to say something. I didn't say anything. So he went on.

"Here's the deal. I need a cat-sitter a couple of nights a week. Maybe three. A few hours each of those nights, maybe between eight and midnight. The cat's name is Brat. He's not a problem, except he keeps bothering me when I'm working on my laptop. I'm a writer. He seems to be infatuated with the laptop screen. When I lock him in another room, he starts screeching. So that's what I need a cat-sitter for. You get it? I'll be at my laptop making a living, and Brat will be entertained by you, hopefully, in another room."

"Where is your place?"

"I have a loft on the Bowery. Just south of Houston. I thought ten dollars an hour would be fair. And an extra ten for the cab home. That would come to fifty dollars for the evening. Is that acceptable to you, Miss Nestleton?"

Usually, I wouldn't consider it immediately acceptable. Just on general principle. But times were bad. "Are you air-conditioned, Mr. Montag?"

"To the hilt."

"We have a deal."

"Good. Tomorrow night?"

"Fine."

"By the way, I never used a cat-sitter before. Am I supposed to provide food for you?"

I laughed. "No, not really. A piece of fruit would be nice, though. And something cold to drink."

He gave me the address and said that I should not worry at all about Brat—except for his laptop fetish, he was a delightful creature. Of course I had heard such claims before.

And that was that with the phone call.

I tried to go to sleep. It was a bit difficult. I read some James, but my eyes hurt in the heat.

At a little past midnight, I heard the blessed sound of thunder approaching. Louder and louder. I switched off the ceiling fans. The storm hit. Sudden and furious. The heavens opened. Wind and water whipped through my large windows.

As quickly as the storm came, it left. And in its wake was silence and cool.

I drifted off into sleep.

Sometime close to dawn, I woke with an itch on my left leg. At least at first I thought it was an itch. But then I realized it was a bug crawling from my knee down toward my toe.

I sat up and leaned forward to swat the intruder.

Then I saw to my horror that it was a baby mouse crawling down my leg. I mean a very tiny and very young baby mouse.

Now, intellectually, I love and admire all God's creatures. Rodents included.

But in the real world I had become deathly afraid of them, like the stereotypical dizzy blonde who screams and climbs up on a chair at the sight of a mouse. It happened very suddenly, about two years ago. I don't know why. Maybe some complex reaction to aging. What was really interesting about my newly formed mouse fear was that it only became severe when I was alone or lonely or feeling abandoned by humans.

Anyway, I gave out one of those stereotypical squeaks of horror . . . half moan, half scream, all embarrassing. It would be hard for anyone hearing such a performance to know that the performer, as a girl, had calmly eaten breakfast every morning in a Minnesota farmhouse with clearly visible field mice chattering on a nearby kitchen shelf, looking for sugar.

The baby mouse dashed off me; obviously it now realized I was not its mother. It scooted under the dining room table, where it just stopped and waited by one of the legs.

Crouched on the floor about five feet away from the baby mouse was old Pancho.

He was crouched real low, like a leopard in the grass. If he still had a tail, no doubt it would have been twitching, for his eyes were focused on the prey under the table.

Brave, noble, modest Pancho. He would protect my home and hearth. I winced, realizing I was about to witness the central ritual of the wild—a kill.

The baby mouse realized his or her situation. It remained absolutely still under the gaze of the ferocious stalker, Pancho.

Then the baby mouse made his move. Toward the closet, where there were enough holes around the perimeter to move a regiment of full-grown mice.

Now, I thought. It's going to happen now. I braced myself for the carnage.

Pancho didn't move. He just sat there and watched the little mouse disappear. I felt a sudden rage. I screamed at him: "You coward! You traitor! Why didn't you protect me? Why didn't you *do* something?"

When I realized how ridiculous I was being, I just sank back down onto the Turkish towel and watched the morning light emerge, on the verge of tears, but never getting there.

The next morning I retrieved Bushy from the vet and told him the whole shameful story, saying that his partner Pancho had exhibited extreme cowardice in the line of duty. Bushy did not appear to be surprised.

In the afternoon I went to the film Forum and saw a 1970s comedy, *Welcome to Greenwich Village*. Then I went to an air-conditioned Starbuck's on Spring Street and read Henry James on and off while eating a chocolate chip muffin and drinking two iced coffees. (The refill was half price.)

At seven-thirty I walked the six or seven blocks to the Bowery and rang the downstairs industrial-type bell of Louis Montag's dwelling.

I was buzzed in. I walked up a wide set of concrete stairs to the third landing. Montag was waiting for me at the open door.

"Did you have any trouble finding me?" he asked.

"Not at all," I replied.

He opened the door wide, allowing me to

enter. I was struck immediately by his height—
he towered over me—and his crookedness. His
shoulders were extremely uneven and stooped,
and his elbows looked as if they had been broken and reset. He was dark complexioned with
longish hair for a man his age—he seemed about
forty-five—and he was dressed like a SoHo
painter, in sandals without socks, a ripped
T-shirt, and carpenter jeans of great age and
disrepair.

He didn't look at me when he spoke; his eyes
seemed fixed about an inch to the right of my
face.

The loft was quite nice; sparsely furnished,
freshly painted, and heavily air-conditioned.

It was divided in two by a single set of sliding
doors. One entered into the work area. From
where I stood I could see the sleeping area
through the doors. That was where, I supposed,
I would be entertaining the cat. It looked large
and comfortable.

In the work area, where I was standing, there
were two long tables meeting each other at the
corners. On them were two desk computers and
a laptop, along with a printer, a fax machine,
and a bewildering array of phone equipment
which spilled over onto the floor.

One wall was essentially a bookcase.

And one wall had a hodgepodge collection of

blown-up book covers, hung with abandon in no particular pattern. Some were framed and others were not.

They were obviously the covers for different editions of the same book. And when I got close enough to read the title—*New York by Night*—I realized why the name Montag had resonated in my head with a gentle tickle.

Montag and Fields were the authors of this rather famous guidebook to the New York cultural underworld, if one could call it that.

"Would you like a drink, Ms. Nestleton?" he asked. I liked his formality. He asked the question almost with a bow. And he had one of those pleasant New York accents—soft and gruff at the same time.

I could see the tray he had set up on the sink counter in the small kitchen. These lofts all had tiny, open wall kitchens, put in when the spaces were converted from industrial use.

"Not right now."

"Well, please sit down," he suggested.

There were several chairs in the work area. But they all seemed to be knockoffs of the old elementary school chairs, with large folding arms. I smiled at the lack of options and sat down. "I'd like to see Brat now."

He replied: "I'm afraid he's not here right now."

"What?"

"Oh, there's nothing to worry about. He'll be here in a short while. The walker has him."

"You have a çat-walker?" I asked, incredulously .

"Yes. Brat needs to get out. He's hyperactive. Someone usually walks him from about four to six. Today the walker was a bit late."

"On a leash?" I asked. I was starting to get a bit suspicious. Was this man just eccentric, or dangerous?

"Oh, no. Brat is carried to the park on Forsythe Street in a carrier, then let loose in a fenced area."

"I see."

"But why don't we act as if he is here," Montag suggested. "Just go into the other room and make yourself comfortable until he gets back. And I'll start to work."

Why not? I thought. I got up and walked toward the open part of the sliding partition.

"By the way, Miss Nestleton, I'd appreciate it if as part of your responsibility you answer the phone and doorbells while you're here."

"'Fine. Is there an extension?"

"Yes."

I walked inside. The air was even cooler in this part of the loft. And there was a large, very comfortable easy chair with a standing light right beside it. I sat down, luxuriating in the coolness, and began to read a James tale called "The Altar of the Day."

After the first page, I kicked off my shoes. My feet were still not visible for the simple fact that I was wearing my long Virginia Woolf summer dress—a dull white flax affair that made me look like a lissome, ghostly wraith of indeterminate age stalking the downtown streets.

Time passed. The cat did not return. I put the book down. I heard the man working. I began to get more and more anxious.

What if there was no cat? What if this whole thing was a setup? A way to lure me there? Why? Rape? Murder? Who knew?

At nine o'clock I resolved to just walk out fast. And then the buzzer rang.

Montag called in: "That must be Brat. Could you get him?"

I was greatly relieved.

I walked to the door, fumbled with the latch for a bit, and then swung it open. I saw something yellow.

And then I felt a terrible pain on the side of my head.

And then—well, just blankness. I was no longer there.

Sometime later, I opened my eyes. I realized I was lying on the floor, half in and half out of the open doorway.

My vision was going in and out of focus. The

front of my dress was soaked. I didn't know whether it was blood or spittle or vomit.

I couldn't see a cat.

However, I could see Mr. Montag. His hands were tied behind his back. A rope was embedded in his neck. He was swinging from a light fixture, back and forth, like a metronome. But then he faded to black.

Signet

Selma Eichler

> "A highly entertaining series."
> —*Carolyn Hart*

> "Finally there's a private eye we can embrace..." —*Joan Hess*

MURDER CAN COOL OFF YOUR AFFAIR
0-451-20518-9

MURDER CAN UPSET YOUR MOTHER
0-451-20251-1

MURDER CAN SPOIL YOUR APPETITE
0-451-19958-8

MURDER CAN SPOOK YOUR CAT
0-451-19217-6

MURDER CAN WRECK YOUR REUNION
0-451-18521-8

MURDER CAN STUNT YOUR GROWTH
0-451-18514-5

MURDER CAN KILL YOUR SOCIAL LIFE
0-451-18139-5

To order call: 1-800-788-6262

Who Invited the Dead Man?
Patricia Sprinkle

Whether handling customer calls at the Yarbrough's Seed, Feed, and Nursery or close calls while solving crimes, sixty-something Southerner MacLaren Yarbrough knows how to charm her way through anything.

When a local man is found murdered at her husband's birthday gala, MacLaren sweet-talks clues out of affluent matriarchs, shady drifters, and even a disgruntled parrot to uncover the roots of the crime.

"Sparkling...witty...a real treat and as refreshing as a mint julep, a true Southern pleasure." —*Romantic Times*

"Engaging...compelling...A delightful thriller." —*Peachtree Magazine*

0-451-20659-2

To order call: 1-800-788-6262